AF506657

SHADOW OF THE CRIMSON THRONE

Sami Youssef

Copyright © 2026 Sami Youssef

All rights reserved

The characters and events portrayed in this book are fictitious. Any similarity to real persons, living or dead, is coincidental and not intended by the author.

No part of this book may be reproduced, or stored in a retrieval system, or transmitted in any form or by any means, electronic, mechanical, photocopying, recording, or otherwise, without express written permission of the publisher.

ISBN-13: 979-8-9946361-0-7
ISBN-10: 8994636107

Cover design by: Sami Youssef
Library of Congress Control Number: 2018675309
Printed in the United States of America

For the ruthless immortal cosmos.

CONTENTS

Title Page

Copyright

Dedication

Chapter 1   3

Chapter 2   12

Chapter 3   20

Chapter 4   25

Chapter 5   33

Chapter 6   44

Chapter 7   53

Chapter 8   58

Chapter 9   73

Chapter 10   86

Chapter 11   100

Chapter 12   110

Chapter 13   125

Chapter 14   138

Chapter 15   149

Chapter 16   160

Chapter 17   171

Epilogue   179

Acknowledgement   187

Books By This Author   189

The Awakening

Part Two

Shadow of the Crimson Throne

By

Sami Youssef

CHAPTER 1

Tare'Envel Burns

Tare'Envel burns. Smoke curls into the night sky, thick and choking, carrying with it the stench of charred timber and scorched flesh. Dark clouds spew ash on the unfortunate people trapped beneath.

Leaning against the balcony railing, Kestus' fingers stung as they tightened around the cold iron as he stood watching like a gargoyle. From the heights of Rhyden's manor in the High City, he had a clear view of the destruction below. The Undercity—*his city*—was drowning in blood and fire. The streets, once alive with the pulse of gang rule, now belonged to King Alikhan and his Crimson Guard.

A sharp pain lanced through his side as he shifted, his body still weak from the wounds of the past seven days. His ribs ached, from deep bruises, a stark reminder of how close he had already come to dying. He had spent a week locked inside this manor, forced to heal while King Alikhan's soldiers carved their way through the city. His teeth ground together. He should have been down there—fighting, running, doing something. Instead, he remained here, above it all. Watching. Waiting. Helpless.

Below, the streets churned with movement. White-cloaked soldiers marched in formation, their boots striking against stone with a mechanical precision. They weren't simply hunting; they were purging. Movement from a nearby market caught Kestus's gaze. A squad of the Crimson Guard was dragging a man into the center of the street: one of the last remaining lieutenants of the once powerful and mighty Starstride.

Torren the Shining Scar.

The Starstrider was forced to kneel. Blood dripping from his temple, his breath was ragged. The scar he was known for, shown bright in the light of the guard's torch. It stretched from ear to ear, across the bridge of his nose, just below his eyes, like a spider's web visible at just the right angle.

A second guard stepped forward, his voice ringing across the square.

"By order of King Alikhan, all who defy the Crown will repent and those who do not beg for the King's forgiveness shall suffer. For treachery is a disease.

One that must be cut from the body." Looking down at the Shining Scar the guard readied his blade. "Will you beg for your King's forgiveness?" His voice was soft; nevertheless, he held no hope for the Starstrider.

With one eye closed, Torren looked at the guard, blood and snot covering his face. Streaks dripped down and around his lips. With a blow, he spat the gunk at the towering man before him. "Until my final stride through the-"

Without hesitation, the soldier drove his sword into Torren's gut, cutting him off. The Shining Scar gasped, body jerking against the steel, a choked groan slipping through clenched teeth. Blood spilled in thick rivulets, staining the cobblestones until it pooled at the soldier's boots. Standing there, waiting until the very last moment, the guard let Torren's body slump and fall back off of his sword onto the ground. Then, wiping his blade on his cloak, he added the streaks of blood next to the splatter Torren had spat at him and stepped over the body as though the dead Starstrider were no more than refuse.

Fingers curling, Kestus' knuckles went white as he squeezed the railing. His anger turned from boiling hot into a cold steel.

Starstride was shattered.

The Crimson Guard had made examples of the named men—anyone with rank or loyalty to Tyven had been hunted down. Those who survived were herded into warehouses, their fates uncertain. Some whispered of forced labor till death released them. Others claimed the Hushed lingered in the dark corridors, ensuring their pains and suffering would last eternally. Whatever the truth, Starstride had been dismantled, piece by piece, methodically and without remorse.

Tyven would have stopped this, if I had just given him the bracer. I should have listened to you, Jeret. I should have trusted you both.

Nevertheless, Tyven was gone. The Seventh Star—Starstride's most prominent inn and base of operations—lay in ruins, reduced to blackened rubble. If the Blade had survived the assault, he had vanished so completely that even the King's spies could not root him out. Without Tyven, his growing empire had crumbled. What had once been a gang, then a guild, was now nothing but broken pieces of what was once a pillar of the Undercity.

Despite Starstride's demise, RavenHood still fought. With every beak and talon, they called for Alikhan's blood. Yet, they too would meet their end soon, for their numbers were too few. They set traps and ambushes that slowed the Crimson Guard; like knives in the dark alleys of the Undercity, they struck. It wasn't enough though. They couldn't turn the tide on their own. Every victory cost them blood they could not afford to spill; mainly spies and assassins, they struggled to hold their own against the near limitless soldiers King Alikhan possessed.

After the fall of the Seventh Star, it became apparent that Knife Point had fractured in two. Some swapped their allegiance and bent the knee, swearing themselves to the King. This new and treacherous menace came to be known as "the King's Decree." They wore the white-and-gold of the Crimson Guard, bearing weapons and armor handed down from the soldiers, too expensive for anyone in the Undercity to afford. Named men were given the King's *honour* and rose to knighthood, allowing them to act as hounds loose in the High City, silencing anyone who dared to whisper against the Crown.

Those too loyal or too dimwitted to leave Knife Point still followed Ironfist. Seven Fingers was a solitary remnant of Ironfist's most loyal bruisers, and a captain now, who struggled to keep the trusted few in line. They were too scattered and too reckless. As always, Knife Point struck with rage rather than reason, becoming more like fodder hurled at the guard's shields than soldiers of a cause.

And, just as quickly as they had appeared and spread, the Hushed… had vanished. The inhuman, guttural scream he had heard scraped against Kestus' thoughts, and their silence pressed heavily on his chest. Their absence did not mean safety as so many voices claimed. No, Kestus knew, it was the promise of something worse to come. Rhyden would remind him every day to stay sharp, to always be alert, for the noble also knew worse things lay ahead. The rest of Tare'Envel didn't know the part the Hushed had played in the destruction of the Undercity. They had no idea, and they weren't afraid enough.

Kestus exhaled sharply and turned his gaze to his wrist. The Shiftscape Bracer clung there, its weight both an anchor and a burden. The strange artifact bit into his skin, the gemstone at its center was no longer a deep, roiling black. Instead, it had dulled to a clouded grey, as though the life inside had begun to grow, but currently dormant, waiting. That both made Kestus feel closer to the artifact and frightened at not knowing anything about the odd relic.

Rhyden had funded the heist to steal the Shiftscape Bracer. He had wanted this artifact and in the end, when it was sitting within his grasp, he let Kestus keep it, telling him almost nothing about the damned thing other than it was a key and held great power.

A key, huh? I do not want to see what you open. Since, we met everything started to crumble around me. You got Jeret killed. You saved my life, a couple of times. I want to hate you. And yet, I still think you and I are the only ones that can fix this fecking mess. Looks like we are in it until the end then...

The Shiftscape Bracer gave its usual hum through his body. Running a hand through his wavy hair, he closed his eyes, basking in the sensation. Instantly he could sense that slow thump, as if a second heart was fueling his veins.

Behind him, Aegis stood silent as ever, a statue of steel. Wood shavings drifted to the floor as his steady hands worked on a small carving. His armored bulk was larger than nearly any other man, and yet somehow his presence was even larger. It filled every space and every corner when he was present. The visor of his helm caught the dim glow of the lanterns that lit the early morning. He never spoke. Never removed his helmet or even a glove. A week had passed since Kestus had awoken, battered and half-broken, watched over by the iron-clad figure, and he still knew nothing about the man. Not his face. Not his voice. Not even his purpose. Regardless, the knight had a gentle nature. Kestus felt safe with Aegis by his side.

After seeing what had happened to Torren, the burden of it all and his current situation reached its peak. Kestus slammed a fist against the railing, pain flaring white-hot through his arm spreading up his body and right into his ribs, making him flinch. "I should be down there."

Aegis listened; still he did not stir, nor did he say a word. He just kept working, scraping away. Then, after a long moment, there was a steady sound of steel boots on stone as the iron guardian departed, his presence vanishing like a shadow swallowed by the manor's halls.

Jaw tight, Kestus exhaled through his nose, chest heaving. He needed answers as to why all this was happening. He had stolen from King Alikhan, yes, but the destruction and murder of countless innocents in the King's own kingdom all because of it? That was beyond belief!

Rhyden, while distant and quiet, was Kestus' best chance. He had been weaving threads in silence, slipping between nobles and cloaks, whispering alliances in the dead of night, building an alliance with those of the High City. If anyone still carried a plan to fight back, it was him.

And if Rhyden didn't? Then Kestus would carve his own path. The injustice the King had brought forth would not go unpunished.

Eyes filled with pain, he turned from the burning city, letting the glow of fire and the falling ash fade as he stepped deeper into the shadow of the manor. The Undercity bled, its gangs were broken, its people shackled, but Kestus Quickhand wasn't finished. Not yet.

CHAPTER 2

Hope Plotted Out

A loud commotion reverberated throughout the manor's walls. Hearing the noise, Kestus rushed downstairs to see what was happening, his mind racing with possibilities. Were they under attack? Was this another training simulation Aegis was distracting him with? To his surprise, his host had returned, covered in blood.

Lord Rhyden Tuo sat slumped in one of the high-backed chairs, his usual poise on the verge of cracking. Blood seeped through the cloth, staining his fine white shirt. His expression remained un-readable, though his keen eyes—dulled by pain—slipped toward Aegis as the armored man wrapped him in bandage after bandage.

With the final knot tied, Aegis shook his head and stood up, his gauntlets covered in noble blood.

Waving him off, Rhyden scowled at his guardian. "I don't have a suit of armor like you, or a magic bracer like Kestus. Some of us are just regular people. I wasn't trying to get stabbed, it just happened!"

Kestus leaned against the stone wall, arms crossed. "With an injury like that, you shouldn't exert yourself so much. You should be resting." He was pleased to finally repeat the phrase he had heard all too often over the span of the past few days.

The sky outside loomed over the dying city as the moon's hazy glow struggled to pierce the rising smoke. Only a few strands managed to slip through the window, casting shadows across Rhyden's face.

With a sharp exhale, a half-smirk tugged at the nobleman's lips. "And yet, here I sit, bleeding on my favorite chair." His gaze shifted to Kestus. "You know better than most, we don't have time for rest."

Kestus pushed off the wall. "What happened? Who possibly could have landed a blow like this against you?"

"An unfortunate disagreement with one of Alikhan's minions. It appears the Hushed do not like when men try to glimpse at what they are hiding." Rhyden's voice was dry, the effort of speaking clearly cost him. "Alikhan's grip is tightening and not just in the Undercity. I met with some of your shadowed friends and a group of nobles. There is going to be a moot for the remnants of the gangs. I was not able to get all the details before we were attacked, unfortunately, which means, I will have to meet them at a new location now, wasting even-"

"You're in no shape for anything!"

Readjusting himself, Rhyden sat taller, his entire demeanor sharpening as though the pain that held him moments before had been banished. His tone carried command and the air of nobility.

"Which is why *you* will be going in my place."

Surprise rippled through Kestus. His fingers twitched toward the bracer hidden beneath his silken sleeve. It was everything he wanted and yet he didn't like the sound of it. "You want me wandering the Undercity?"

"You're a thief from the Undercity. Sneaking around the Undercity, no one will notice you unless you want them to. You are a master thief after all. Besides, Ironfist called the moot. The gangs that remain—the ones still resisting Alikhan—are gathering to form an alliance. Yes, I want you down there, gathering an army. Everyone must be involved if we are to succeed."

"Ironfist?" Kestus scoffed, bitterness coating his tongue. "You mean the same bastard who bent the knee to Alikhan? He sold out the Undercity. Knife Point was responsible for the fall of Starstride."

"He bent the knee after he rebelled against the King. He stole from the nobles and had his hand cut off for it. That is not loyalty. There will always be bad blood between Alikhan and Darron. While I agree Ironfist is no more than a thug, he holds no allegiance to the so-called King. It was only a matter of time before the dog slipped loose of its chains. You know as well as I that the new faction that now follows Alikhan is but a fraction of Knife Point... The King's Decree is nothing but lost souls clinging to a hope of salvation that only exists while we live. Alikhan would have them disbanded and hung as soon as he knew their use was at an end."

Aegis marched back in, his armor no longer stained with blood. Taking the silken shirt offered by the steel giant, Rhyden donned the blue fabric, the wound beneath concealed from sight.

"Ironfist is no fool," Rhyden continued. "At least not in this sense. He knows that Alikhan will dispose of the King's Decree. Right now they are useful —thugs to shame the nobility, while keeping the image of his Crimson Guard clean. This gathering will create a unified Undercity, a unified cause— maybe one with the power to bring back his turncoats."

"Even if that's true, why would anyone trust him? Before the heist, Knife Point was brutal enough to put everyone on edge. No one will agree to this,"

Kestus said, turning back to the window, his gaze pulled toward the ruined city.

Rhyden's shrug carried the burden of inevitability. "They do not have a choice. If the gangs keep fighting one another, they will certainly be crushed one by one. Starstride was the first, and clearly they will not be the last. The Undercity is bleeding. The nobles are too afraid to act. Without numbers, we will lose everything." He paused, his expression tightening. "If you can gather the gangs, then I can gather the nobles. Only then will we have a real chance at this."

"A chance at what?! Look out there!" Kestus' voice cracked, his shoulders sagging as his eyes lowered to the bracer. "The city will never be the same... because of us."

Stepping to his side, Rhyden looked down at the thief. His voice dropped lower. "Kestus, I understand what you are feeling. I, too, have watched my home burn. I have seen the ones I love beaten and slaughtered." Rhyden's mask broke, revealing a brief pit of sadness, then hardened with resolve as he continued. "But we have not lost yet. There is still time for Tarc'Envel. Meet this contact and I will find others in the High City. Sebastian Vale seems to be listening to me. If we have him, we have the nobility. Those are our first steps."

Kestus narrowed his eyes, spitting the words with

scorn. "So you want me to play diplomat for the criminals while you rally the rich?"

SMACK!

The blow landed before Kestus even had time to blink. He gasped, stumbling to catch his balance. Hand pressed to his cheek, he spun on his heel to glare at Rhyden, the taste of copper blooming in his mouth.

The faintest shadow of amusement twitched across Rhyden's lips. "Sir Kestus Retchet, people are dying. More will continue to die with or without you. Now, you can play diplomat for the criminals, as you have been asked, or you can stay here with Aegis while I stop Alikhan's machinations from bleeding this city dry—watching like a fly on the wall, alone and unable to do anything."

Tonguing his cheek, his jaw already swelling, Kestus considered Rhyden's words. He didn't trust Ironfist—not even a little. Regardless, if the leader of Knife Point was serious about fighting back, he couldn't afford to ignore him.

Sighing in resignation, Kestus asked, "Who's the contact?"

Turning from Kestus, Rhyden's eyes traced the rich furnishings of his manor, his expression caught somewhere between pride and weariness. "Filko Sharp-Eye."

Kestus let out a short laugh of disbelief. That changed everything! Filko wasn't just another informant—he was the leader of RavenHood, a man who saw more than he ever revealed. If he was involved, then this wasn't some desperate gamble. This really was a chance at something.

Rhyden is right… This could work. Filko and Ironfist, together? They could pull the Undercity together.

Knuckles tightening into a fist, Kestus watched the smoke rise above the city. It no longer looked as if it were an omen, rather, it looked to be the perfect shroud for a thief to move unseen. "Where does Sharp-Eye want to meet?" Kestus asked.

"One of the few places people of your nature can still get into. The Dry Spell." Kestus closed his eyes, lips curving in the faintest smile. The sound of Rhyden's boots faded into the manor, his voice following in echo. "He may already be there, with the time we wasted debating. Best hurry and catch him."

Kestus turned to see Aegis waiting, silent and immovable, holding out his cloak—the one Tyven had given him—sewn back together where fire and blades had torn it apart.

Caught off guard, Kestus' words came out softly. "Thank you." His hands gingerly accepting the gift. The cloth felt smoother than before, lighter somehow.

Aegis answered with only a nod, the subtle grind of metal-on-metal from his armor breaking the silence.

Looking closely at the material, the stitching was nearly imperceptible. Kestus drew the cloak around his shoulders, adjusting the fabric so it hung properly. It fit perfectly. "I'll see what Sharp-Eye has to say. But, if Rhyden's wrong and this turns out to be a trap, I expect you to come get me."

Aegis shifted to the side, allowing Kestus to pass.

From deeper within the manor came Rhyden's short, wry laugh, ending in a sharp inhale. "You have a talent for surviving traps, Sir Kestus. Just don't make a mess of the negotiations, and you will have done what was needed."

Already stepping forward, Kestus ignored Rhyden. If they didn't find a way to fight back, there would be nothing left to save.

With a steadying breath, Kestus pulled up his hood and let his hand rest against the Shiftscape Bracer, his fingers absently tapping the artifact. Its unearthly beat quickened at his touch. As he stepped into the blood-stained night, the shadows closed around him with the embrace of an old friend.

CHAPTER 3

Déjà Vu

The city had changed. No longer did the crooked streets and curtained doors bring charm to the place he called home—instead they made it feel closer to a cage. The small trappings had always hung in the place of windows or doors in hopes to ward off evil, only now there was no escaping the danger. everyone had become playthings for Alikhan's wrath.

King Alikhan the Stern... the name of a damned bastard. How could you do this to us? To your own people? What could matter so much to you? Whatever it is, no matter the cost, I will stop you!

His chest calm, despite the tightness in his ribs, Kestus moved swiftly along the rooftops. By now, he considered the bruise an old wound. Aegis and Rhyden were relentless teachers, adding newer ones as they taught him the sword. Still, the pain in his ribs was a small price to pay—Clubface would never harm anyone again and if a bit of tightness here and there was all he had to suffer, it was worth it.

The streets below were unrecognizable. The King's fury, his Crimson Guard, and the new King's Decree, had left homes broken and crumbled, with scattered rubble that blocked alleyways and swallowed sidewalks. Checkpoints clogged every major road, each one manned by soldiers clad in stark white armor—what little remained visible beneath layers of dried blood. *The Crimson Guard*. They were more ruthless and savage than any gang, even at Undercity's worst. Their name had little to do with the colors they wore; rather, it was their horrifying methods of coloring their cloaks that made the name infamous.

Civilians were shuffled forward, forced to present papers, coins, or favors to pass. Those who had none were dragged away. No one needed to guess what came next. It was clear. The city was being bled dry—a dying corpse, just waiting to fall.

Seething as he watched, Kestus stood above it all, moving like a cat across the uneven rooftops. He stalked the guards, his blade ready, wanting to strike, wanting to bring peace, except he knew his goal was to save everyone. Risking being caught now...

Stay focused. You are getting close. I can't just jump in

The Dry Spell wasn't far. It lay at the edge of what used to be Starstride's territory: a small, unassuming tavern. Once, it had been a rare gem in the Undercity, a neutral ground for thieves and schemers where gold and secrets changed hands in whispered deals. Now, it stood under constant watch. A destination only fools occupied.

The King had yet to burn it down like he had with so many other dens. He left it alone for now, forcing people to believe there was a glimmer of hope. "Enjoy it now. The tavern could be gone tomorrow." Or, "Maybe, King Alikhan isn't after us. He just wanted those gangs." Of course, none of that was true; they were just the lies people tell themselves to make the fear go away. What it did, was create a melancholy that hung over the district and a reluctance to stand against the King's will. People are unwilling to protect others, if they are always trying to protect themselves.

Once a familiar tavern, The Dry Spell held nothing but pain for Kestus. Only a span of days had passed since his last visit, but it felt as though years had gone bye. Here was where everything began. Had he never stepped through the door, what would have happened to Tare'Envel?

A patrol of the Crimson Guard marched through

the street below.

Smiling to himself, Kestus knew the guards couldn't stop him, they were an unnecessary precaution. Despite the constant patrols, anyone worth anything in the Undercity knew how to slip into the Dry Spell undetected. The place was made for thieves.

The last time he pushed through that warped wooden door had been to meet Jeret.

A job. That's what he told me. A promise of coin and power. Only, neither of us knew what we were really agreeing to.

Jeret had given him the details—the plan to steal the Shiftscape Bracer from King Alikhan's castle. Kestus had been cautious, skeptical, yet not afraid, at least not afraid of the King. Back then, the worst danger he had to worry about was getting caught.

Now, everything was different.

He had the bracer; still, nothing else had gone as planned. Jeret was dead—brutally murdered by the Hushed. The city was at its breaking point. And Kestus knew he was the reason. Starstride had become a target, even though *Kestus* was the true prize. If the King got hold of him, whatever sick plan Alikhan harbored would come to fruition. That knowledge helped ease Kestus' mind. Had he done nothing, Tare'Envel would most likely have been swallowed whole by now.

Perched on the edge of a decaying parapet, overlooking the entrance to the Dry Spell, Kestus forced himself out of the growing pit in his chest. Filko was late. The agreed time had come and gone. His eyes scanned the rooftops, unease coiling in his gut. His fingers beat against his knees.

Did Rhyden have bad info? This feels wrong. I'm calling it...

Just before he could rise to his feet, a figure draped in a raven-feathered cloak glided across the adjoining roof and slipped through the tavern's attic door.

About time.

CHAPTER 4

Meeting In A Crowded Room

With the grace of a feather, Kestus dropped from his perch, landing in a soft roll, then pressed himself against the tavern's wall. The muffled bustle of voices spilled through the stone and wood. There was an abundance of patrons inside tonight. That boded well for his secret rendezvous—more faces meant more chances any onlookers would forget his.

Peering through a streaked window, Kestus studied the common room. No guards. No uniforms. Only thugs and broken people.

Moving quickly, he went around the back and slipped through the kitchen door.

The scent of burnt meat and spilled ale filled his lungs—an aroma that felt oddly familiar, almost comforting in its filth. The cook, sleeves rolled to the elbow, was too frantic to notice him, chopping vegetables at a furious pace for the stew bubbling beside him. From the next room came the loud voices of a roaring crowd, their laughter and shouts competing with the clattering of mugs.

Hardly bothering with stealth, Kestus briskly stepped to the doorframe and looked in. A rowdy group of fishermen were drinking, empty mugs at their table and ale-frothed mugs in their hands. Their joy mingled with the smoke-stained beams of the ceiling. Their weather-worn clothes and sunburnt faces told him they had brought in a good catch and by now they had already drank through their earnings.

Moving further into the main room, Kestus scanned the area, searching for his feather cloaked contact. He spotted a figure near the corner table, back turned to the kitchen, their hood drawn low. The cloak hid any details of who they were; nevertheless, the posture was tense, watchful.

Roles being reversed I would look more of a twitching wreck if I were one of the most wanted men in all of Tare'Envel, sitting with my back pointing toward an open tavern. Luckily, I get the side closer to the wall.

Warily, Kestus approached, his hand resting on the pommel of his dagger—the ornate weapon he had plucked from King Alikhan's vault, the emerald gem in its hilt still gleaming faintly in the tavern's lamplight. The subtle tap of his fingers on the metal kept him at ease but ready. This could very well be a trap.

As he crossed the hall, a few glances bore into him, lingering on the Starstride sigil woven into his cloak. The room seemed to hush. The patrons shifted away, careful not to be mistaken for allies of a dead faction. To the Undercity, Starstride had fallen. To Kestus, it was still a banner of defiance—one this city needed now more than ever.

Maybe I should have tried to be more subtle. This was supposed to be a secret rendezvous after all…

Sliding into the seat across from the cloaked figure, Kestus's breath caught. It wasn't Filko Sharp-Eye.

The name passed his lips as if it were a secret.

"Ellia!"

Surprise painted his face like mud struck up from a rain-soaked street.

A grin swelled on Ellia's red lips as she pushed her hood back. "Took you long enough, Quickhand."

Letting out a sharp breath, the tension in his shoulders loosened as he pulled his chair closer. "Ellia." The name tasted sweet on his tongue, twisting his features into an involuntary smile. "I'm glad I wasn't the only one who got out alive."

She leaned back in her chair, the old wood groaning, her dark raven hair tied into a simple ponytail. "After I saw you slip into the castle, I met up with Renny and we escaped before the lockdown." Her eyes drifted away for a moment, turning somber. "When I heard about Jeret, I was worried you'd finally gotten yourself killed."

They held each other's gaze. A flicker of relief crossed their faces, fragile, yet undeniable, in the storm of everything else. For a moment, the world around them didn't exist. This was the life Kestus missed. A hard life, filled with its own dangers, but one that held possibilities.

The urgency that Rhyden had filled him with rose up, clutching those pleasant thoughts and choking them out, a suffocating smog that encompassed his brain.

"What can you tell me about the past days?"

Ellia filled him in on what had happened in the seven days since breaking into Alikhan's castle— the city's descent into fear, the gangs splintering, the Crimson Guard tearing through the Undercity-hunting anyone suspected of resistance. Blood had covered the streets.

Absorbing every detail, Kestus nodded as he listened. Listened to everything Ellia said and everything she didn't as well. There was one name he hadn't heard.

"What about Tyven? Has anyone seen him since the fall of the Seventh Star?"

Ellia's expression darkened.

"He's dead. Everyone that was there that night is. That's where Knife Point's segregation was made public. That's when the Hushed revealed themselves as living nightmares and aligned with the bastard King..."

Kestus clutched at his chest, feeling the words as if they were a blow to his ribs. "I had hoped... That was the last time he and I... that's where he and I, we separated...feck. Somehow it made sense when we did."

"They say Captain RosenThorn claimed the kill." Her voice was quiet, anger pressing deep lines into her brow. "They boast she put a sword to the Blade himself. Pierced his heart with her *Blade of Thorns.* If I ever got close enough." She scoffed. "I know exactly where I'd put a blade in her."

Tyven was too careful, too clever. If RosenThorn got to him, then nothing in the city was safe anymore. Kestus clenched his jaw, looking away. Racking his brain, he tried to recall if he had seen anyone matching her description that day. Then it struck him.

"The Crimson Guard wasn't there. It was only Knife Point and the Hushed..." A smile tugged at his lips. "Knife Point had new equipment but they definitely didn't have soldiers aiding them like they do now."

Seeing the glint in his eyes, Ellia knew she had to be the voice of reason.

"Kes, he's dead. They have his sword, *Starfire*. Even if the Guard is lying about who killed him, none of Starstride made it out. We both know Tyven wouldn't let his people die for him to escape."

The warmth faded from the air between them, drowned beneath everything they had lost. The glint of hope vanished along with Kestus' smile.

Exhaling, Kestus steadied himself, stopping his restless fingers from tapping through the table. There would be time to grieve later. Tare'Envel was bleeding, and he had come here with a purpose.

Now, there was just one more thing for him to do, avenge Tyven.

I'll add it to the list then.

"Ironfist." The name alone carried enough heft that Ellia knew to move on.

Straightening in her chair, her shoulders sagged with the souring of her mood. "It's a good plan."

"What is the plan?"

"Gathering the gangs for a strike against the King," she said tightly, her voice low burning beneath restraint. "There's no way the Crown can stop us! If all of the Undercity rises against the High City, we outnumber them! We'll be able to push them back and then they'll finally know our pain. What it's like to see your protectors turn against you. It wouldn't be long for the nobles to see the King for what *he is*, after he abandoned them to save himself." A fire sparked in her eyes. Ellia balled her fists tight, trying to hide them in her lap, unable to fully suppress the rage inside.

Remembering his talk with Rhyden, Kestus wondered if this was how he had sounded—an over zealous youth with naïve ideas of grandeur.

Rise up and take down the King! The Undercity isn't enough. It sounds silly now hearing it from somebody else.

"Do you trust him?" Kestus asked, crossing his arms and leaning back.

Placing her hands on the table, Ellia scratched at her thumbnail, avoiding his gaze. "No... My uncle told me stories of Ironfist when I was young. His cruelty scared me then, and in his older age it has fermented into something even more sour. He's like a rye bread, but one that the dough fell in dirt first so it was never good to use." Closing her eyes, her fingers stilled; she threaded them together before pulling her arms back to her sides. "Still, he is making a stand, and he's asking for our help. Trust or not, we can't do this without him... And Kes... we need you too. The Shiftscape Bracer you carry—the

King wants it. That's what the Guard searches for in the checkpoints. We have to—"

"I know." Kestus nodded. Offering a friendly smile, he didn't want to make her feel like she had to plead for his help. "When and where is the moot?"

"Tomorrow, when the moon is at its peak. We will be meeting at the Tartrap…" Ellia saw Kestus flinch at the name.

Rubbing his eyes, he laughed into a hand, "We're gathering everyone who stands against the King in an abandoned tar warehouse that even has 'trap' in the name. Okay. Why not?" Taking a breath, Kestus let it go. "I'll be there. Still, El—you have to admit this sounds like a ploy."

"Quickhand… all nights are dark, the stars are what light your way. Remember the cloak you wear, the relic you protect, and bear the burden." Standing, she gave a long look at everyone in the tavern. "See you there." She spoke over her shoulder. Pulling her hood up, Ellia slipped into the back room, leaving through the kitchen.

Biting his tongue, Kestus watched the RavenHood fade away. His fingertips absently rubbed the cloth of his cloak.

Bear the burden…

CHAPTER 5

Sir Philip

The air in the tavern grew thick with tension as Kestus dwelled on what Ellia had said. He lingered in his chair, eyes on her empty seat. The sound of clanking mugs and merry tales dimmed, while the volume of voices rose. Anger grew with each conversation, the patrons at the bar shouting for more ale, slamming their fists on the counter. The barkeep snapped at their demands, his voice cracking with frustration. Near the front of the inn, a group of men argued so fiercely they blocked the entire entrance, their shouts carrying above the rest.

Something wasn't right.

Instincts prickling like needles along his spine, Kestus looked around the room, without raising his head. Ellia had left only moments ago, slipping through the kitchen. Now a fistful of cloaked figures pushed their way out of that very same direction.

"You can't be back here!" the cook was shouting, his voice thin against the swelling roar of the crowd.

The barkeep didn't hear him—or was just ignoring him entirely—for a different group of cloaked men had already seized him by the shirt. The barkeep's fury boiled over into a screaming match that split the tavern in two.

Venom began filling every face, spitting words sharp enough to draw blood. Kestus' eyes flicked across the room, from one group to the next. His stomach was sinking. The Dry Spell was no longer a tavern—it was a tinderbox ready to burst into flame.

It's definitely time to go.

Kestus tried to push himself to his feet—only to be slammed back into his chair by a burly hand the size of a mallet. His breath caught, his ribs protesting the sudden impact.

"Feck..." he hissed, realizing too late that the trap had already closed.

Beside Kestus, a heavy-set man groaned with the chair he filled. He wore chainmail and a breastplate bearing the King's crest, half-hidden beneath a dingy cloak of the King's white and gold. The color was so off the white looked to be more of a filmy cream and the gold a bronze yellow. His hands were scarred and burned, palms thick with callouses.

Clearly, he was accustomed to violence—inflicting it and surviving it.

"Quickhand, is it?" A heavy sigh escaped his lungs, followed by a deep sniff before he cleared his throat and spat on the floor beside him. "I'm Sir Philip Brod of the King's Decree. Once known as Bloodclot. Good to meet you, lad. These are my associates." Sir Philip's hand tapped the table and then gestured toward at least a dozen men, watching as they began surrounding the table.

Feck. There's a good amount of them and Bloodclot is pretty large too. He probably won't go down easy.

"I couldn't help but notice that bracer there on your arm. That is the property of our King. If you kindly hand it over—" A violent cough cut him short. He held the table as he doubled over, gasping for air. The cough traveled from deep inside of Sir Philip, scraping the lungs and yanking the air along with it. Drool lined the corners of his mouth as he wheezed and sat back upright. "Hand it over, and I'll make sure the RavenHood brood we got outside hangs. I'll be transparent: you both are going to die. If I were in your shoes, I would see death as my final freedom. It's how you die that I control. Any commotion on your end, and all these fine men will get a say in what happens to *her*. And not all of these men share my same ethical limitations."

For the first time, Sir Philip looked Kestus in the

eye. No longer puffing or heaving. They stared at each other good and long, memorizing every part of the other's features. The rage pouring out from Kestus made the knight grin. Jagged and stained teeth flashed behind his cracked red lips. "I bet we can make this work. Just us named men." Sir Philip mused. Then he shook his head and continued. "Well, that's the old way of thinking. I'm sure a *named* man like yourself can handle negotiating with a fine knight like myself."

The worn leather felt soft beneath Kestus's tightening grip. The ornate dagger was already in his hand, unsheathed and eager for its bloody business. He had to get through these men to get outside. Ellia had been followed, and he had no idea if she had escaped in time.

This was so stupid to meet here! What the hell was Rhyden and Filko thinking!?

First though, he'd have to cut through this half moon of the King's thugs. A feat that great was going to require something more from him.

"Tell me. What tipped you off?" Shifting to the edge of his seat, Kestus leaned in, ready to spring.

Eyes narrowing, Sir Philip mirrored the movement. "With all due respect, what idiot wears a Starstride cloak in such an obvious place? Haven't you heard? Tyven the Blade is dead, just like the rest of his gang. The Shining Scar was just put to the sword early this morning. For such a skilled thief, you do not seem very bright." He smirked. "Now, before you do something stupid, take a mo—"

Flinging the table toward Sir Philip, Kestus pounced at the man nearest to his left. Surprise flashed across the thug's face a split second before the pommel of Kestus' ornate dagger shattered his jaw. Teeth spilled across the floor as the man collapsed.

Kestus didn't stop.

Momentum—that was the lesson beaten into him over the last week by Rhyden and Aegis. Battle was always about momentum. Follow each step with another step. That's how smaller forces overtake larger ones, and It's how he would win today.

The next man was two paces away. Closing the gap in one, Kestus was close enough to kiss him. Eyes centered and head cocked back, he drove his forehead into the thug's nose. The cartilage crumpled beneath the impact of Kestus' skull, blood bursting across his face as the thug gargled a scream and fell heavy like a tree. The thought of Broken Nose—now No Nose—flickered across his mind.

Engage and disrupt. If they can't think of attacking, you gain the upper hand. Right. Next step. Keep moving.

A scraping sound caught Kestus' attention. He turned just in time to see a chair hurtling toward him. He dove forward, cloak snagging on the frantic legs of the flying furniture. A sword slashed past him, cutting through the Starstride blue and grazing his back.

Eyes wide, Kestus felt his heart hammer against his ribs. The pulse from the Shiftscape Bracer throbbed against his wrist, a silent command.

It was time.

No. Not yet! I can keep going.

Another sword tried to skewer him, as he slid across the floor. Knife in hand, Kestus sliced at hands reaching for him but there were too many. The group of attackers were closing in, each kicking or trying to grab hold of him. He had lost the momentum. There was no chance he could fend off the King's Decree laying on his back.

Now, it was time.

In the briefest of moments where time naturally stopped, Kestus let out a breath. Steadying his nerves, he focused on the melodic thrumming in his veins. The rhythm had grown so natural, it was almost as if it were the beating of a second heart, off tempo with his own.

Using his Shadow Step, the power inside of the

Shiftscape Bracer ignited.

The world began shifting and warping. Swaying lantern flames caught as the fire was mid-flicker, held there-burning for all eternity, trapped in this space of time. Darkness deepened across the floor, connecting all shadows into one, the wooden boards beneath drowning in a pitch-black tide.

Like light through glass, the shadows bent around Kestus, transforming the environment, allowing him to step—not forward, not back, but through the Dry Spell. One moment he was flat on his back-surrounded on all sides—the next, he was up and circling behind them, looming as though he were death given form.

The advantage was his once again.

By his count, there were ten of the King's Decree left. Not enough to stop him. Moving fast, calculating his breaths, striking pressure points, and disarming weapons, he used their numbers against them. When he was done, they would lie crumpled and groaning, still alive, but broken. He wouldn't kill them. Not like this. They were traitors and yet, Kestus knew what fear could do to a person.

Fear was a sickness that festered in the soul and drove good people to do terrible things. These men *were* traitors; of that there was no doubt. Still, they had once been members of Knife Point. They were once loyal to someone besides the King. In fact they directly opposed the throne. This group of people may still be the worst, down right, no good, gutter trash that's ever walked the Undercity—nonetheless, Kestus understood that the will to survive changed people, and the only choice King Alikhan gave his people was to stand with him or die.

Suppressing a grimace, Kestus walked up to Sir Phillip. The knight's mouth hung open, a layer of spit frosting his lower lip. Up close, the thief could see the knight in excruciating detail. Dark blue veins slithered beneath his skin, styes marked his eyes, and skin tags covered the creases of his nostrils. Ingrown hairs added to the markings across his face, where the stubble of his beard had begun to grow in patches. His armor didn't fit well and was leaving red spots that could just be seen where the chainmail exposed his skin. He held himself primarily on his left foot, the injury he had taken to his right knee at some point in his past, apparent by the way his bone had set at an awkward angle. In his hand, he held tight a hammer, rusted and dented. This was clearly the tool he had earned his name with. Once Bloodclot of the Undercity, he was little more than a fragment of the man he once was.

Tightening his grip on the ornate dagger, Kestus' eyes widened. To his surprise, the blade had already left a scratch just beneath Sir Philip's eye.

If I don't end this knight's life, more will die. Crippling him may work, but it'll have to be more than just a knee. That clearly wasn't enough last time. Besides, the way he is already pushing his body, despite the wear and tear, means I'll have to make it really last...

Twisting the dagger in his hand, he slashed!

Avoiding arteries, he severed the knuckles of Sir Philip's hands. Then he cut the tendons behind Sir Philip's knees, slicing at all the areas his armor couldn't cover. For a time, while they were in the bracer's *Shadowrealm,* the knight would be able to do nothing except suffer.

The bracer hummed as Kestus released its power, the magic fading from his veins as he pushed toward the kitchen. He exhaled slowly, grabbing hold of the archway as the world screeched back into fluidity around him.

The group of the King's Decree were thrown into chaos. Disarmed, they began stumbling into each other. A few of them were mid-swing and unable to stop their attacks, their blades drove into allies or struck against walls as they slammed point first into them.

Sir Phillip's battle cry morphed into a scream as his bulk collapsed under Kestus' blade. The hatred in his voice gave way to excruciating pain, traveling from his ankle to the top of his spine, flooding into his skull. The disbelief in his groan made Kestus chuckle. The giant man struck the wooden floor with a thunderous impact, sending tremors through the Dry Spell.

"Fecking QUICKHAND! I'll kill you! I'll fecking KILL YOU! Nowhere will ever be safe for you—"

The curses continued raging, but Kestus had already moved on. Slipping through the kitchen door into the alley, his mind was racing, fixated on one thought.

Ellia!

He hurried into the back alley just in time to see the last of her attackers slump into a pool of blood.

Four of the King's Decree. All dead.

The final man had been stabbed again and again and again, long after he had stopped moving. Ellia stood over the body, her chest heaving, her blade dripping scarlet.

Without a word or even a look, she brushed past Kestus, her breath still ragged and stepped back into the inn.

"Ellia—" Her name died on his lips just as a cold rain began to fall alongside the ash. The scene of death before him was covered in a glistening shroud.

Standing in the rain, fists clenched tight, Kestus stared at the blood washing its way into the gutters.

He knew what she was doing. He also knew she was wrong, except he couldn't bring himself to stop her. The King's Decree was destroying families. Perhaps this was the lesser of the two evils. So, he waited outside while Ellia carried out the dirty work he didn't have the stomach for. Screams and shouts grew louder, drowned out as the rain began to fall harder. Its steady pattering blocked out the sounds from inside as well as his thoughts…

Finally returning, she slumped against the doorway. No words were needed, and none were shared. From the corner of his eye, he saw her raise her hood and slowly draw closer—her eyes watching a spot far off.

"We're being watched." She whispered over her shoulder.

He could feel it too.

"We can split up and try to lose them, but I don't know how many there are," Ellia continued.

"I have a place we can hide out."

Studying him for a moment, she reached up and brushed the dripping wet curls from his face and pulled his hood over his head, letting her hand linger a second longer than necessary. "Lead the way, Quickhand."

CHAPTER 6

Safe For Now

The rain blackened their path, silencing the guiding flames. With a familiar ease, Kestus moved quickly through the winding streets. Taking detours and looping back and forth through streets and alleyways, he listened for the echo of pursuit, watching carefully for the faintest sign of movement. Ellia kept close to his heels, her steps light and nearly imperceptible in the pitter-patter. The two had slipped through most of the Undercity by the time dawn began to stain the horizon with a smoky orange and pink. Their hunters had fallen behind, no trace they had ever been there at all. Regardless, Kestus still felt the weight of unseen eyes pressing against his back, as though the city itself had begun to stalk him.

By the time they reached his safehouse—a tucked-away shack near the city's edge and the closest thing he had to a "home"—he knew something was wrong. It wasn't hard to guess. The door sagged, barely held by its hinges, the frame splintered as though pried apart with brute force.

Someone finally found it.

With a sigh, he gently nudged the door inward, trying to keep it from falling over.

Inside, the destruction of his few possessions hit even harder. The room was gutted. Papers lay torn and scattered across the floorboards. His notes on King Alikhan's castle, presumably gone. Drawers overturned, tools broken or missing. The single chair he kept, its legs and back broken beyond repair. His mattress had been stabbed through and left to rot.

They must have come searching for me after I stole the bracer. Who would think that I'd be brainless enough to try and hide something so valuable here? Damn, I really liked that chair.

Stepping in behind him, Ellia wrinkled her nose at the stale bitter air. "You must bring all the girls here," she smiled to herself and nudged a broken piece of something with her foot. "Quite the sight." She placed her dagger beneath a charred scrap of paper, tilting it to the light to examine the parchment better, before letting it fall. "And you think this place is safe? Sort of gives off kill room vibes. Tight space. One door in and out. Seems pretty easy for them to trap us inside and surround us." She looked up at the arched ceiling. There were no windows anywhere, just old swollen wood.

With a grumble, Kestus shot Ellia a glare, all though he didn't protest. She wasn't wrong.

Crouching, he began gathering scraps, then stopped.

What was the point?

Whoever had been here already took what they thought mattered and ruined everything else. The remnants left behind were just that—fragments of old heists and half-finished thoughts. Nothing worth fighting for. Nothing worth saving.

It's all gone. And now that it is, did any of it matter? Kestus Quickhand-Master Thief. What do I have to show for it?

Drifting further inside, brushing dust and splinters from the old broken chair—Ellia used papers and rubble to even out its stubs, before settling into it with a casual air, as if the wreckage amused her. Kestus dragged the table against the broken door, propping it the best he could to make a thin veil of security,

Finally, he sank against the opposite wall, arms folded across his chest, his muscles feeling bruised and tense. This place had never been as safe as he believed and now that too tugged at his thoughts.

His fingers found the Shiftscape Bracer beneath his sleeve, absently tracing its edges. Exhaustion settled heavy in his bones. Moving his fingers felt like raking water. The toll of the artifact had become relentless. Training with the bracer along with Rhyden and Aegis had made him faster, sharper, more dangerous. Despite that, the burden of it pressed harder upon him each day, reminding Kestushe was no master of its power.

Not yet.

Ellia's gaze flickered toward his cloak. She watched as his fingers moved underneath the fabric, ever so lightly swaying one way and then the next.

"Did you use it?"

As if woken from a dream, Kestus started. "Yeah." He paused, there was no point in denying it but something inside him wanted to keep it to himself. "They sent at least a dozen of the King's Decree. I guess you know that. You were there…" Shaking his head. "I was able to fend off some at first but they got around me pretty fast—there were too many."

Slowly, scooting further onto the chair's edge and reaching out, her fingers brushed against his and the Shiftscape Bracer. The movement told him she would have done the same.

He couldn't feel her touch through his cloak, but the proximity between them sent waves of heat coursing through his veins. She moved in closer, slipping off her seat, her hair spilling forward like shadows, hiding her expression.

"I didn't expect it to feel warm," Ellia said gently, her voice soft as satin. "Like it's alive."

"When I first touched it, it was cold and then it sent a jolt like a thunderbolt through my body." Swallowing, his throat dry and his breath shallow, he sat as she continued to trace the etchings through the fabric. Her hand lingered as she held him, creeping closer, careful of the splinters scattered about them. When her emerald eyes met his hazel ones, they became transfixed.

Staring at one another, neither moved a muscle. Her eyes traced the dark waving curls that rested across his forehead, hanging just above his eyes. They were as still as paintings, until she rubbed the growing scruff across his cheek.

The smooth touch of her skin caused a smile to form on Kestus' face. His smile reflected in Ellia's, her eyes seeming to widen-pulling Kestus in even deeper. The emeralds grew into an endless cave filled with twinkling gems. Lines of black surrounded her eyes adding to the effect. Her skin held no blemishes, even beneath the thin layer of white paint she wore. She smelt of flowers and sweat. The concoction was intoxicating.

Without thought, his free hand found hers and he leaned in.

She met him halfway.

The kiss started slow, uncertain. She flinched at first, but did not pull away. Her swollen lip from the fight made it raw—like kindling. Igniting something inside, the pain fueled her. Their kiss deepened, an unspoken release of everything they had held back: the fear, the exhaustion, the loss, and a passion that grew hotter with every touch.

They would let it take over, consume them until the sun rises and life comes knocking.

Suddenly, the door slammed against the table with a CRACK!

In an instant Kestus leapt ahead of Ellia, ornate dagger drawn, crouched and ready to strike. Ellia stood just behind him, blade pinched between her fingers, poised to throw.

A gust of wind pushed the door again, causing it to smack the table once more.

Closing his eyes, Kestus released a long sigh. Rising, he slid the knife back into his belt and glanced over his shoulder—Ellia's smirk matched his.

"To kill the wind, one must take its breath away," Ellia mused.

"To be truly breathless, one must be dead." Kestus looked at the curve of her lips, darker now since their kiss.

She tilted her head, studying him with an unreadable expression. Then turning, she moved to lay in the remains of his bed, pulling her raven-feathered cloak across her body. "I give you one task, Master Thief: ensure no one steals my life tonight."

"My Lady RavenHood." Kestus bowed slightly before taking the chair. The moment had passed. Ellia struggled to get comfortable. Kestus, his gaze lingering on the door, his fingers absently tapping his knee, was resolute in the fact he would not be sleeping tonight.

Master Thief. *Looks like I'm not the Beggar Thief after all.*

Morning came quickly, its welcoming glow glittering and reflecting off broken glass and shards of mirror. Kestus startled awake, not realizing he had closed his eyes. The chair had left a deep ache in his back. He had been slouching against it and somehow had been lucky enough to topple out of the wobbly piece of rubble.

Ellia was already fastening her boots when he stirred. Glancing at him, her expression seemed softer than usual.

"I need to go.," she said. "Filko needs an update on what happened. He's probably worried the plan went wrong after I didn't make my way back last night. Knowing him, he is probably assembling Talons and a group of Ravens to come hunt for me."

Trying to get to his feet gracefully, Kestus gave a nod. He instantly regretted it when his neck spasmed from the movement.

Seeing him wince, Ellia strode over and massaged the knot. "They have to hear we have support from the High City—that not everyone agrees with Alikhan's genocide. They need to know we have Rhyden and that we have you on our side..."

"Right, don't want him to worry. I also need to head back to Rhyden and let him know the plan." Turning, Kestus cupped Ellia's fingers in his hands and kissed them. With her boots she stood just below his nose. At this angle, however, she stood above him her chest level with his head. Smiling down at him, she pulled her hands away and resumed gathering her things. "So, I won't see you until the summit?"

"I'll be there."

For a moment, words hung unspoken between them. Then, without another glance, she slipped out the door, the table doing little to stop her.

As light as the wind, you fade away. A wisp of life

taken, 'til another day.

Staring at the space she had left behind, Kestus sat lingering in the silence. Yesterday, the emptiness inside him had felt like a wound, hollow and consuming. Now, something else pressed against it—something sharp, alive, and unfamiliar. Their meeting had shifted him, filled him with a purpose he had not realized he had been craving. Perhaps this was the change he needed.

After all, the plan was not entirely absurd. It was simple—dangerously so—and often the best-kept designs were the ones stripped of flourish, hidden in plain sight.

He let his gaze drift across the room one final time, memorizing its corners, its shadows, its familiar stillness. Then, with a slow breath, he turned on his heel. Time to let go of this place. Time to become what the Undercity needed him to be. It was time to return to Rhyden's manor.

CHAPTER 7

Breaching The High City

The High City loomed above, as if it were a spider weaving its web. In the distance, buildings peered down like gargoyles, watching the masses swarm their gates. Polished stone streets, now marred by the growing chaos, greeted those who still believed its walls provided security. The air carried the sour tang of sweat, smoke, and blood, mingling together, making every breath feel thick in the chest. Keeping to the shadows, Kestus remained calm and focused as he approached the checkpoint barring entry into the market district. Sneaking into places he wasn't supposed to be in was his profession after all.

Stay vigilant and there's nothing to fear.

A line of merchants, travelers, refugees and desperate commoners stretched down the street. Their faces hollow with exhaustion, they all were waiting for their turn to be questioned, shaken down, or turned away. With the loss of their homes, many from the Undercity who wished to stay out of the fighting relied on the nobility to show mercy. Mercy was scarce. Remaining neutral was growing more difficult; no one was certain if helping someone else would bring the King's ire.

With the influx of Voy'Din refugees seeking aid, the Crimson Guard had reinforced the barricades with wooden carts and steel pikes. Their armor caught the torchlight in a dull, menacing glow, while the dried blood streaking their cloaks showed just how fiercely these soldiers clung to power.

Looks like these guards only care about showing the King's fist to their people. Men of war. They forgot who they were supposed to be protecting. These people are willing to risk death for scraps of the noble's mercy.

He spotted one of the guards slam a man against a wagon, his gauntleted hand crushing the breath from the merchant's lungs, while he continued to bark demands and accusations at the stunned man. The merchant fumbled for his coin purse with trembling hands, shaking his head-clearly trying to focus his vision-and held it out. He bowed, his face nearly touching the ground, as if offering his life.

"You don't have enough." The guard growled, searching the purse. Pulling the merchant to his feet, he shoved him toward another of the Crimson Guard, as he pocketed the coins and dropped the ragged purse to the ground. The second guard grabbed the collar of the man's shirt and hauled him behind a canvas partition.

A scream split the night air, as shadows depicted what happened behind the canvas.

Cries rippled through the line of waiting people as two more of the guards began dragging the man's wagon away. The sound of weeping spread through the crowd, hopeless and hollow sobs.

Knuckles white, Kestus let out a breath and unclenched his fist. He had no coin to bribe his way through and he had no intention of being dragged behind the canvas. Using his Shadow Step wouldn't work either, the distance was too far. He would have to sneak across.

His eyes flicked to an approaching wine cart, barrels stacked high with crates of fruit squeezed between them. The merchant steering it was already arguing with the coin hungry guard, his frustration just barely hiding the tremor in his voice.

Be careful what you say, merchant. If they haul you away, I can't risk intervening.

Before he could second-guess himself, Kestus hurried. Slipping beneath the cart, he pressed himself flat against the wood and embedded himself. The faint scent of spilt wine and rotting fruit stung his nose.

No one noticed.

All eyes were on the merchant. The crowd gaped—parents pulled their children closer, others averted their eyes. Unaware of all of this, the merchant continued arguing.

Ignoring the man's ramblings about how important it was he get into the Ivory Row to sell his goods, the coin hungry guard narrowed his eyes. There was a sound like gravel shuffling underfoot that caught his attention toward the back of the cart.

Come on let us through!

The latch of the wagon swung open, spilling a head of cabbage on the ground. The entire wagon shook, as a boot thudded against the wood planks right above Kestus.

Voices continued to argue.

With a grumble, the guard grabbed a bundle of grapes and hopped from the cart, slamming the wagon's back shut behind him. Dangling the fruit above his head, he took a bite of one and gestured before speaking, "Move along."

"Thank you, sir!" The merchant's voice changed from a belligerent fool into a squeaky boot licker. "May you continue to uphold the King's honor. I'll offer you a discount if I see you at the market!" The merchant urged his cattle forward into a trot.

"Come on!" The guard screamed, waving the next family in line over.

The road was rocky at first, where the High City and Undercity met, then a smooth ride. If Kestus had been laying in the wagon he would have been able to fall asleep beneath the clearing sky.

Once the checkpoint was a safe distance down the hill and the cart reached the start of the market district-the wonderful and grand Ivory Row-Kestus rolled free into a side alley and began shaking the trip from his cloak. Wine had dripped onto him, as every bump in the road jostled the barrels.

Aegis is going to kill me when he sees this thing. The stains alone...

Before he could slip deeper into the High City streets, shouting erupted from the markets.

CHAPTER 8

The Symbol Of Judgement

The Ivory Row was on fire.

Keeping close to the buildings, Kestus crept from the alley as he moved toward the rising sound and dancing flames. His cloak was drawn tight, bundled to dull his outline, the better to blend with the night. In his fine sweat-stained white shirt and dusty black trousers—slightly damp but mostly clean given the circumstances—he could almost pass for a merchant or lesser noble caught in the chaos.

Let's just hope no one sees the Starstride sigil. Damnit Kestus, why'd I grab this cloak?

Moistening his cracked lips, he struggled to believe what was happening.

The wide stone avenue had become a war zone in its own right. Nobles were ripped from their homes, shops, and carriages. This was worse than the barricade. Thugs in the King's colors—

the King's Decree—moved like a pack of starving hounds, dragging their victims into the streets. Families were hurled onto the marble steps of their own estates. Their cries split the night as parents and children were torn from each other's arms.

Slipping along the darkness, Kestus remained on the outskirts, careful not to draw attention.

What the feck is happening? King Alikhan is going after the nobles and merchants now?

Then a phantom of a man stepped out. Kestus' blood chilled as he stared at the figure that anchored the carnage.

The towering man stood at the center of the street. Masked and silent, he stood watching, as an unshakable tree might watch a forest. Even with the mask covering half his face, Kestus could see the ruin beneath—old cuts and scars covered the flesh. The mask was of a skull and marked with a crimson hand.

At his side, he carried a long polearm with a banner bearing King Alikhan's crest. Its fabric twisted, dancing in the wind, looking down on all around it. His other hand rested on a dagger Kestus knew instantly. The hilt was burned into memory—simple and reliable, it once was his own.

"Old Trusty…" Kestus whispered, his throat tightening. "Looks like you found your way back to me.

I'll come for you"

A merchant woman in yellow silk robes suddenly was hurled to the ground before the masked figure. Trembling and covered in tears-her painted makeup smeared-she tried to crawl away. His gaze, slow and deliberate, fixed upon her, he remained planted and still-watching her sob.

"We gave you a chance to prove your loyalty." he growled, his voice grinding like stone. With a savage kick he knocked her onto her back. "But you chose to follow traitors over your own king!"

"Please d-don't hurt me!" No longer fleeing, she sat on hands and knees, submissive to his authority. "I'll do whatever the King wants. I have done nothing w-wrong. I've done nothing wrong! NOTHING!" Tears continued to pour down her face.

Jolting forward, Kestus was ready to act—when an arm blocked his way.

The woman rose to her knees and continued to beg the masked man. The words being spoken were lost to Kestus in the roar of the marketplace. A blade flashed, blood spilt across the stone, the woman grasping at her throat—shaking her head side to side in disbelief, her hands unable to stop the inevitable. After a moment she slumped forward.

I hope you find peace…

Tracing the arm to who had stopped him, Kestus found Rhyden's scowling face. The noble's gaze fixed on the beast of a man dragging the woman toward the center of the market.

"Do not intervene!" Anger dripped from his mouth. Kestus had never seen Rhyden like this. Despite his words, the thief could tell that Rhyden found it equally difficult not to rush head first into the King's Decree. "Their actions are a ploy to make anyone resistant to Alikhan's rule reveal themselves. They have the numbers and an attack now could ruin all that I have worked for. For now we wait."

"We can stop this!" Kestus hissed, pulling at Rhyden's arm.

Rhyden's lips were pressed into a thin line, his eyes narrowed. Then he spoke, "No. There's a chance this will be exactly what we need."

Lowering his arm, Rhyden strode down the Ivory Row, following the King's Decree soldiers as they pushed deeper into the market district. His words left Kestus dazed.

What we need?' How the feck could this be what anyone needs? I should do something if he won't.

From the shadows, Aegis strode forward, peeling away from a grey painted shop where he had been leaning. Despite being clad head to toe in gleaming armor, Kestus hadn't heard or even noticed the ironclad guardian.

Without a word, Aegis placed a sympathizing hand on Kestus' shoulder. Then with a firm nudge, he urged him to follow Rhyden.

The guardian's cloak was slung over his armor. Its crest was of no land Kestus had ever seen. A crescent moon with a sword piercing the lower curve, and a shining crown as the pommel. The image meant nothing to Kestus, yet it reminded him of the Starstride emblem he wore on his tattered cloak. This clearly meant something to these men, for Rhyden wore one too. Together they stood defiant, the last remnants of dead clans.

Keeping his eyes forward, Kestus forced himself not to look at what was happening around him. Despite the division between the High City and the Undercity, he would never wish this punishment on anyone. He had never known his mother or father; nevertheless, seeing families torn apart felt as if it opened a new wound inside of him. It was wrong, cruel, and inhumane.

No man should be allowed to call himself "King" if he is willing to do this to his own people.

From the corner of his eye, Kestus saw Rhyden tense. Within a breath, Aegis already had his gauntleted hand loosening his sword in its scabbard. If Rhyden struck, Aegis would be at his side in an instant.

"No! Not him. I need him!" Rhyden growled through clenched teeth, crossing the sidewalk and stepping onto the main road. He gripped a lantern pole, using all his strength to hold himself back.

Scanning the crowd, Kestus couldn't see who Rhyden meant. No face stood out, no familiar ally. It was another of the many moments he was aware Rhyden was far more capable than he appeared.

Then someone Kestus did recognize came into view. The noble's fine violet coat was torn, his face already bruised and bloodied as if he had been beaten and tossed down a flight of stairs. The masked man was dragging him by the ankle. After discarding the noble woman's corpse he had moved on to his next victim.

Lord Sebastian Vale.

Despite his youth, he held substantial influence in Alikhan's court. Sebastian inherited control of several textile and mercantile shops as well as the largest of garrisons from his late father. His fabrics were the main source of cloaks and jerkins for the Crimson Guard as well as servicing most of the nobility in all fashions.

Every sworn lord to the King had to devote men to the King's army, as a tribute to their loyalty. Despite sending half his forces to serve in the Crimson

Guard, Sebastian Vale's army outnumbered most of the other noble families.

Rhyden had been trying to meet with Sebastian—one of the few nobles still willing to listen, willing to oppose the King's brutal rule. He was the thread that held Rhyden's fragile plans together. If he were to die here, any chance of winning the rebellion would too.

Led to a makeshift podium at the center of the lavish street, made from shop stalls and crates hastily thrown together, Sebastian was pulled to his knees. Blood slid down from his temple, pooling beneath his chin, dripping onto the white stained wood.

The masked man crouched low, his grin stretching beneath the teeth of the skull. He whispered something in Sebastian's ear, causing the noble to bare his teeth. Sebastian moved to stand, until a boot sent him plummeting to his side. The masked man didn't help pull him up this time, but gestured to Sebastian to stay where he was. Cowed by the beast, the noble dropped his head and lay where he was—looking up at the crowd.

Knowing his prey would listen, the masked man lifted up his polearm high and let its flag unfurl in the cool smoky wind. Voice cracking like a whip across the square, he yelled to the gathering people.

"Come now! Come forward. Witness the King's

judgment!"

Striding closer to Sebastian, his sneer curled into something more intimate. "You nobles. You think you can whisper behind locked doors? Shuffling your little coins in the dark, scurrying away to the corners, hiding in the shadow. Did you truly believe the King would not notice? Not care? Did you think that we wouldn't find you?!"

Lifting his chin despite the blood streaking his face. Sebastian's voice was steady, though his breath seemed to rattle in his chest.

"We have done nothing wrong! We are nobles of Tare'Envel. Nobles that serve the King! We only want what is best for the city. For our home! You cannot look at what's happening and believe this to be right. To be just!"

With a low and cruel chuckle, the masked man drove his polearm into the podium's top with a re-sounding crack, sending splinters gliding through the air.

"We are the King's Justice! The shadows of the throne. All of you should have listened to your King! Should have proffered yourselves before his feet! Any blood on our hands is because of your own actions."

Grunting, he took a heavy step forward and kicked Sebastian, sending him sprawling across the podium. The noble struck his head against the edge of the stage, a sharp thud that silenced the murmurs in the crowd. Disbelief at the brutal punishment could be heard from gasps through cupped hands—or ugly sobs. Dazed, Sebastian tried lifting his eyes just as the masked man grabbed a fistful of his hair, wrenching his head to the side.

Pulling out *Old Trusty,* he began straddling the man. With the slow, deliberate ease of a butcher at work, the brute began carefully slicing through the noble's ear.

Screams tore through the square. Sebastian's legs flailed like eels, flapping against the wood—unable to reach his attacker. Arms buried beneath the brute's bulk, he tried scratching at the podium, causing splinters to flake off.

With a vicious shake, the masked man dropped Sebastian and stood, holding up the severed ear for all to see.

"Listen to me now," he mocked the noble.

Body trembling, Sebastian coughed out a curse. "Go to hell!"

Grin widening, the Masked Man tossed the ear onto the cobblestones, where it landed with a wet slap.

Raising the knife again, Kestus' knife, the monster gestured Sebastian forward. "You first."

"Well done!"

Clap. Clap. Clap.

The voice carried through the tense silence, drifting through like a raft in the ocean after the entire crew was swallowed by a wave. A figure approached through the crowd, each clap of their gauntleted hands echoing like steel against stone.

Clap. Clap. Clap.

The masked man straightened at once, sliding his knife back into its sheath. He bowed low, hand raised in salute. Two fingers to the brow, the opposite arm drawn stiffly across his chest, fingers hanging loose to symbolize vines of thorns.

Walking to the front of the podium, her white silk cape sweeping over the bloodstained stones, was Captain RosenThorn .

Unlike the rank-and-file Crimson Guard, her armor bore engravings of roses, her shoulders crowned with cruel iron thorns. She was shorter than Kestus had expected; even in her armor, she would only come to his nose. The visor of her helm was lifted, revealing beauty. Her nose was straight, with high and sharp cheekbones. She had a cleft chin, similar to her fathers, yet gentle in its regality. The fire made her armor shine as if she were a beacon, standing as a hero before these people.

Two of the King's Decree hurried forward, each helping lift her onto the podium.

Looking down at the bleeding lord, her eyes flickered to the masked man before turning away from him with a visible revulsion. Her gaze found Rhyden's. A small tweak lifted her lips, and she gave him the faintest nod. Like snakes, her eyes slithered to Kestus. In that mere moment, he could feel her measuring him—taking him in, weighing his worth. This was the King's daughter. The spear he threw, the sword he struck with, the voice he used to shout; she was the King's harbinger..

With a flourish, and the grace of a dancer, RosenThorn twirled toward the crowd, raising her arms above her head, and began clapping once again.

"What a show!" she declared, her voice loud but never shouting.

A few uncertain people in the crowd joined her, clapping hesitantly. Nodding her head, she brought her arms down and kept clapping until the entire crowd followed.

With a single wave, she silenced them. The market fell quiet, as unsure of her being there as Kestus was.

"This is not what OUR King—my father—wishes for his dear Tare'Envel," she declared, pointing to

Sebastian Vale and clenching her fist. "This man speaks the truth! Many of you are nobles of our wonderful kingdom." She knelt, helping him to his feet, unbothered by the blood splattering her armor as she took his hand. "We all want what is best for this city—not just the High City, but the Undercity as well."

Someone scoffed from the crowd then went silent as if struck from a crossbow bolt from RosenThorn 's hard gaze.

"I understand your skepticism. After seeing, after experiencing what you just did, this must be tough to swallow. What is happening now may seem as if your homes are under siege—"

"Because they are!" Another voice shouted from the throng. The person shied away before being spotted —an act that proved useless as the shadows of the market danced with motion. The Crimson Guard began to line the crowd. Unable to keep himself from tensing, Kestus started taking deep breaths to steady himself as his fingers tapped against his bracer.

They're trapping us like animals! One wrong word, and everyone here could be killed. No matter what the princess is saying.

With a dramatic sigh for all to hear, RosenThorn straightened, resting her hands against the small of her back.

"Seven years ago, the Crimson Guard left this city to defend our kingdom. Seven years ago, I left the people of Tare'Envel, taking our soldiers to fight for our freedom against the Voy'Din. When I returned, I found a fractured city. The gangs of the Undercity, groups that once served our King in keeping a fragile civility amongst the riff-raff—had grown defiant, disrespectful, and drunk on their own power. Our King's castle was ransacked, treasures stolen, the halls defiled. When I left seven years ago, I did not think I took the strength and heart of our city. I believed those attributes were held in the people."

With a shake of her head, RosenThorn looked away, unable to meet the eyes of the crowd. When she raised her head again a fire burned in her eyes. "After seven years, I return to my home—to OUR Tare'Envel—and discovered that these rats, vermin, these vagabonds—stole from the Crown, but also slaughtered our noble citizens! People just like you... and Lord Vale."

She pointed toward the man on the podium, blood dripping down the side of his head, clinging to the polearm embedded in the table top to balance himself. Two of the Crimson Guard stepped forward—cloaks still immaculate, unmarred by blood or dust—and guided Sebastian off the stage. One of the other guards rushed over, inspecting his ear.

"The thieves, following Tyven the Blade's orders, snuck into the King's castle during a religious gathering and murdered nobles in the middle of their prayer. Slitting their throats before their God. Stealing their futures. Leaving their families shattered." Her voice grew sharper, and clenching her fists, she began pacing the stage.

"What kind of captain—No. What kind of citizen— No! What kind of daughter of Tare'Envel would I be if I let that stand? Tyven forced this on you all. He made it necessary for me, for your Guard, to rise up and protect our home with steel!"

Her chest heaving, she paused and removed her helmet. A cascade of straight brown hair tumbled free, falling across the steel and leather of her armor like a banner.

"We do not act to harm you. We do not act to cause pain. Yet, measures must be taken. Action must be delivered. This cannot happen to our city—our people—ever again. The Undercity shall know its place. No longer will there be division between us. We stand as one, united beneath the Crown!"

She raised a hand toward the masked man at her side.

"The King's Decree. Those who stand with our King have been given a chance to show loyalty and devotion. Sir Loss is one of our newest pillars of protection—a shield against the snakes and rodents who poison our streets with doubt and disobedience." The masked man bowed once again. "Only together can we rebuild Tare'Envel. Only together can we root out the rats that have infested it. It was with their help, I stormed Tyven the Blades den of treachery and removed his head from his shoulders!"

Placing her helmet back on and stepping down from the podium, her final words carried over the hushed crowd. The sound of steel scraping leather echoed in the air as RosenThorn lifted *Starfire,* high above her head.

"If you know any of these criminals or know someone else who does, bring them forward. Help us! Together we will cure our sick city. Your protectors have returned home. With your help, I shall storm through every home or den to rid our city of this taint that clings to our bones!"

As she strode through the crowd, cheers erupted. Men and women dropped to their knees, hailing her as if she were already their savior. RosenThorn never once looked back at Kestus and his group, knowing she had succeeded, and achieved exactly what she wanted.

CHAPTER 9

The Awakening

Rhyden was silent.

His boots struck polished stone with a steady rhythm as they walked. The Ivory Row was not far from Rhyden's manor, yet the distance seemed to stretch on. As the group grew further from the market district, the blemishes cleared from the High City. It was easy to ignore the tragedies happening just beyond the sloping hill.

It's easy to ignore and forget what is happening. That is, until they come for you.

When they arrived at Rhyden's Manor, he whipped the door open, uncaring of holding it for the others. Slipping through the towering doors, Kestus forced his stride to match the pace of the lord and the iron giant.

"For such a large piece of metal, you move pretty quick," Kestus puffed, nearly walking right into Aegis.

The manor loomed over the High City, perched like a fortress carved into the bones of the mountain. It was one of the few places that could rival the King's castle, a seat of influence and quiet defiance. Unlike the castle's gilded opulence, Rhyden's manor was sharp and utilitarian. Massive walls of stone rose around it, more suited to withstanding a siege than hosting nobles. From the outside, it appeared stern and unyielding, and the interior echoed that same intention.

Every corridor had been designed with purpose—chokepoints where invaders could be slowed, staircases wide enough for defenders to hold their ground, and heavy doors reinforced with steel. Even the beauty within the polished marble floors, the stained windows, and the sweeping tapestries were framed by that grim practicality. It was less a home and more a stronghold, disguised in luxury.

Kestus was still struggling with the idea of calling Rhyden "Lord." The man was surrounded by all the trappings of power, except the nobility others flaunted seemed to be a weight that caged him. Stern and unbending, yes, but Rhyden was calculating, and even sympathetic, in ways that surprised Kestus. Rhyden was not like the others who ruled above the Undercity. He was what nobility could be —when he wasn't angry.

Inside the sitting room, Aegis stood in his familiar, comforting silence beside the brooding Rhyden. Arms folded, gaze out on the horizon, the golem mirrored the disappointment and frustration that hung in the air. The feeling was different though, as if Aegis was more disappointed in Rhyden's behavior than in what was happening.

Kestus broke first. "What the hell just happened!?" he cried, the words bursting out of him, shattering the silence. "She just fecking blamed everything her father did on Tyven. On the Undercity!"

"It was genius..." Rubbing his eyes with his palms, Rhyden stretched wide and gazed toward the manor's garden that lined the exterior walls. "Have you ever stared out and just thought about how captivating a tree, a branch, or a leaf can be?"

With a deep inhale, Kestus put his hands on his waist. Trying not to wince or shout, he exhaled. "What the feck are you on about?"

"Is it not obvious? I was gaining the support from the nobles too quickly. RosenThorn saw it and tried to eliminate my progress in one speech." With a sigh, Rhyden lifted his leg to rest across the other and, leaning back in his chair, continued. "No one knows about the cathedral. We have no proof beyond our stories. Your story."

"The truth!"

"Words of a thief. The people only know—with

absolute certainty—of the disappearance of the nobles. And now, RosenThorn gave them a story, fed by their prejudices and fears. Anyone who looks down on the Undercity will find it plausible, no matter how false it may be."

"It's a lie!" Kestus burst out, running a hand through his hair.

"Of course it's a lie!" Rhyden stomped, leaning forward in his seat. "But to many of those people out there, it is the truth." Pointing to the window that looked out at Tare'Envel, and went on. "It is the only truth they will accept in their small skulls. Now, with that one act, she made it that much harder to gather more rebels against her father. RosenThorn even made the people accept the ruthlessness of the King's Decree. They saw the violence, saw their neighbors families torn apart, nevertheless, they now have a reason to believe it is just. Turn your neighbors against one another, have them fear one another. Self preservation. Seclusion. It was a brilliant move." Smiling faintly, Rhyden returned his gaze to the garden, as though seeing victory in the distance, even while speaking of failure.

Looking from Rhyden to Aegis, Kestus was at a loss for words. He stared at Aegis, hoping maybe the metal statue would do something, say something, do anything but just stand there!

Then a thought struck him. "If they have to stop us,

that must mean the King is worried. He knows with the Undercity and the High City against him, his Crimson Guard cannot hold us back!"

"Sir Kestus, it does not matter." Steeling his fingers before him, Rhyden drew out every word to ensure his point was clear. "This is all just an act. Subterfuge. None of this is what Alikhan truly cares for. All he needs is blood. Our blood, the people's blood, his guards' blood—it is all that matters. We cannot stop the ritual. Even more so now." Pressing deeper into his chair, the weight of his thoughts dragged him into its cushions. The hope that was there previously was lost behind the clouds.

Frustration rising, Kestus balled his fists. "Why are you smiling then!?"

"Kestus. I understand what you are feeling. Believe me. Aegis and I have been in this situation before. More than once even. I will admit, this time feels different than the other times, and that difference has sparked something inside me I did not expect." Leaning forward, Rhyden looked to his guardian.

Looking at both men, Kestus continued to fume. "Did it spark your will to act? Because I'm just seeing a man with more power than he deserves, sitting here, speaking in circles."

Aegis turned his helm to look at Kestus. The subtle movement was enough to remind Kestus, Aegis was loyal to Rhyden. He was the outsider here, the temporary ally.

Then, looking closer at Aegis, Kestus noticed a shard at the center of his chest. The crystal embedded there glimmered faintly. It was the same gem-like stone in his ornate dagger, more so in color to the one Rhyden carried in his sword, *Des Roy*. He remembered Rhyden once saying it was similar to the Shiftscape Bracer too. Then it hit him.

"Your sword…" The words formed in his mind before he dared speak them aloud.

At the mention of the weapon, Rhyden's gaze sharpened. "What of my sword?"

"You said before that King Alikhan needed the Shiftscape Bracer to complete this ritual, and that I have yet to achieve the bracer's full power. If it is like your sword, then it can absorb more power. Right?" Kestus's eyes lingered on the weapon above the mantle. Almost without realizing it, he was rubbing the bracer through his sleeve. The artifact pulsed faintly beneath his touch, a heartbeat answering his thoughts.

Arching an eyebrow as he studied him, Rhyden shook his head. "No. You are not ready for it."

The fire in Kestus' stare made the hairs on Rhyden's arms rise. He could see something growing deeper in the young thief, something neither of them fully understood.

"What do I need to do?" Kestus demanded.

Without a word, Aegis turned and walked toward the mantle.

"Sir Kestus, the power you speak of—the power the bracer seeks—comes only from death. These shards require life and energy to work, and the more life they consume, the greater their strength. The Shiftscape Bracer draws upon you. That pulsing you feel—that steady thrum through your veins—is the artifact taking a piece of you. Little by little, until you give it what it wants or become a husk yourself."

Rhyden's words shook Kestus harder than expected. He didn't believe anyone could truly understand the sensation. He thought his relationship with the bracer was unique—singular.

"To fill the bracer with more power, you must kill," Rhyden continued. "That is its price."

As if on cue, Aegis returned. In his hand gleamed a dagger, its strange form catching the firelight. He offered it, blade-first, to Kestus.

"What is this?" Turning the metal in his hand, Kestus' gaze shifted between the other men.

Rising and walking to where his sword rested, Rhyden said, "That was once the head of a spear. The metal in both the Spearhead dagger and *Des Roy* is known as *Ever Ore*—a substance rarer than platinum, harder than steel, and worth more than a hundred chests of rubies and gold. Few have ever worked it successfully. The malformed shape of that dagger proves it."

"The feeling... it's different from the bracer." The metal didn't pulse like the artifact bound to his wrist. Instead, it thudded, as if holding a heart in his hand. Each beat sent waves of emotion coursing through him, amplifying whatever he already felt.

Studying the *Ever dagger* more closely, its spearlike point bore the shape of an arrowhead, thicker than any knife he had seen or held before. Dents and uneven ridges marred the surface, evidence of a stubborn craftsman wrestling against an unyielding material. The shaft was long enough for a hand and then flared where the head had once been fixed to a shaft. Its grooves fit neatly against his fingers. Though it was solid metal, the weapon felt soft in his palm, smooth like polished gold, yet far more durable. The broken wood at its base had been sanded flush, leaving no hilt, no leather grip—only raw permanence.

"This can stop the Hushed, right?" he asked, awe in his voice.

Stepping forward with *Des Roy* unsheathed, without warning, Rhyden tapped the massive blade to

Kestus' dagger.

The reaction was instant.

The two *Ever Ore* weapons screamed as they touched, a piercing shriek that vibrated inside of Kestus' chest. The force jolted him backward, his hand flinching so violently that the dagger slipped from his grasp. Before it struck the floor, Aegis caught it midair-blade first—without hesitation, as if he had anticipated the outcome.

"Damnit! What was that?!" Gasping, chest heaving, Kestus shook out his hand.

Rhyden's smile was grim, knowing. "The pain of a god."

"What?"

"The metal is alive." Rhyden explained. "All its pieces were once whole, drawn from the body of a god beyond titans. Porox, Thylarn, even the Blood-ied Vessel, pales in comparison. When the metal interacts with itself, specifically in violence, it re-coils. Then it emits a force like rejection. *Ever Ore* despises harming its own. That reaction, the force, it is something you must learn to endure. Flinch again, and it may cost you, or someone you care for, their life. Do you remember the first time you held *Des Roy?* That faint ringing in your skull, the distant voice you heard?"

Kestus nodded faintly.

Rhyden sheathed his weapon with deliberate care, the leather squealing against the metal. "That was the echo of its memory. Every shard of *Ever Ore* remembers what it was, even in its fractured state."

Aegis turned, departing once more without explanation.

"Why give this to me?" Kestus asked, eyes following the iron knight's retreat.

"You will be heading back to the Undercity," Rhyden shrugged. "You need to meet with Filko and Ironfist."

"I already met with his niece, Ellia," Kestus interjected quickly. "She spoke of the meeting. Rhyden, their plan—"

"Their plan is the best we have," Rhyden cut him off, fastening his sheath to his belt. "Alikhan's designs move faster than we imagined. The Awakening is nearly upon us. I'll secure the nobles. You rally the gangs. Then we pray it will be enough."

"You really think any nobles will help after what RosenThorn said? You should come with me," Kestus suggested, hand brushing the blades at his hips. Destiny seemed to sit in each dagger, waiting for their moment.

Breathing through his nose, Rhyden made the last few adjustments to his gear. His movements were firm, practiced, and filled with the significance of his choice. "No. Quick action is how we stop this threat. I have waited before, hesitated when I should have acted. I will not do that again. I will spare you that pain."

"Fine. But before we depart, tell me..." The words were hard for Kestus to push out. "What really is the Awakening?"

"Damn it. Now you ask. When time matters so much!" Aegis turned his head toward Rhyden, halting mid-step. Rhyden's shoulders dropped with a reluctant sigh. Looking at his friend, his expression softened, weary yet resolute.

"Alright. You've done everything I have asked, Sir Kestus. I owe you the truth." Crossing his arms, he stared up the stairwell, as though the words he needed were waiting somewhere in the shadows above.

"The Bloodied Vessel—your people once called her a fallen deity. A goddess who bled herself dry to guide mankind through the darkness. The other gods despised her, for she gave fragments of godhood to mortals, no matter how small each drop of her blood carried."

Blinking, Kestus remained confused. "This ritual is to bring her back?"

Rhyden gave a sharp shake of his head, his

lips pressing into a firm line before speaking again. "More than that. The Bloodied Vessel is the Awakener. Only with her resurrection can the blood be stirred awake. If Alikhan succeeds, his power will rise beyond any mortal's reach. We cannot allow it. Anyone with that potential is too dangerous." He shot a glare toward Aegis, who remained silent as ever, then exhaled through his teeth. "He knows now. Can we go? We are wasting time." With that, he shoved the door open and strode out, his boots striking the stone with an impatient stride.

Lingering, in place, Kestus' eyes followed the swaying door. His chest tightened. He had a job to do. Still, he couldn't comprehend how it had grown into this, nor did he fully understand the answer he was given. The Shiftscape Bracer had been a dangerous job on its own. But this? A King's ritual, a resurrected god—this was madness.

How can the Beggar Thief stop the King from summoning a god!? The fecking Bloodied Vessel. Porox's tongue, this just keeps getting worse.

His thoughts churned like a storm, spinning through his mind and body, pressing against his ribs, threatening to split him apart. The fear wasn't just outside anymore; it lived inside him, filled him. Too much rode on his shoulders. His walls shook.

I can't do this...

A soft shuffle of armor reached him. Turning, Kestus saw Aegis standing there, the silent golem watching him with that comforting stillness. The figure seemed immovable, a rock that had existed for centuries, watching as the world turned. No sound, no gesture, just a companionable peace. For a fleeting moment, Kestus wondered if time itself had stopped, but no shadows bent, his Shiftscape didn't thrum.

"I thought you left already." he said, voice cracking slightly as he lowered his head. The faint, rasping scrape of Aegis shaking his helm was an answer of itself.

Swallowing hard, the weight of the action pressing into him. "Thank you. I didn't think I could do this alone."

Without a word, Aegis walked toward the door and waited beside it, nearly as tall as the massive piece of wood.

"Oh! Yeah… right! I'll lead the way." Kestus hurried forward, shoving his doubts down, and slipped through the opening.

To his surprise, Aegis lingered behind him just long enough to turn the key and lock the manor doors behind them.

CHAPTER 10

Path Of The Saint

Thinking it would be near impossible to slip back into the Undercity with a shining suit of armor trailing behind him, Aegis surprised Kestus with a grace that defied his bulk. A heavy, dark cloak concealed much of his frame, clipped in precise places to mute the scrape of metal. The fabric dragged slightly as he walked, distorting his profile, while never snagging. Every seam, every cut, had been chosen with purpose: clearly the work of his own hand.

A talented artist.

Kestus couldn't help glancing back at him now and then. Aegis was a walking fortress—faceless beneath his iron helm—and still he moved as if he belonged here. Like a man who had walked these alleys long before, or perhaps one who knew enough of suffering to understand the people forced to live in them.

The morning haze still clung to the soot-stained

stone of the Undercity. Smoke drifted through every crooked alley, heavy and biting, mixing with the metallic tang of blood. The streets were alive with misery: vendors hawking scraps scavenged from the ruin, beggars with hollow eyes slumped against broken walls, and enforcers in white stalked the lanes. Their tunics, jerkins, and cloaks were smeared in crimson, trophies of the purge they were carrying out.

The Crimson Guard were everywhere. Checkpoints sprouting like weeds, each one choking the life from the streets. The King's Decree—thugs draped in jagged insignias—patrolled with equal fervor, pulling citizens aside for inspections that ended in bruises, shattered teeth, or worse. They had taken on the Guard's ritual, smearing themselves in blood to prove their loyalty to Alikhan's madness.

At this pace, it will take us all day to reach the Tartrap.

As they wove through alleyways and broken arches, Kestus noticed Aegis pause. Not out of caution. Out of care. The kind of care a noble rarely showed, especially in Tare'Envel.

Rhyden once told me, Aegis makes him a better man.

Near a collapsed water trough, a child sat trembling beneath a half-burned blanket. Aegis approached without a word, kneeling until his iron frame seemed almost human. From beneath his cloak he drew out a crust of bread wrapped in cloth and laid it gently beside the boy. Then, with the same unhurried motion, he set down something else: a small wooden carving of a knight, smoothed by countless passes of a blade. The detail was delicate, exact. Days of patience poured into a gift most would overlook.

Lingering in the shadow of his hood, Kestus watched. The boy's eyes lifted, wide with disbelief, then fell to the carving. He clutched it to his chest as if afraid the stranger might change his mind and snatch it back. As if it were a trick. The boy was not used to such kindness. Aegis simply pressed a fist to his chestplate, slowly methodically patting his breastplate, then rose. For a heartbeat, he stood above the boy, still patting his chest, the helm's gaze unreadable.

The child hesitated, then mirrored the gesture with a shaking hand. The boy's confidence grew as the two of them became synchronized.

With a slow nod, Aegis slowed his thumping. The boy copied his gesture, returning the nod. And just like that, Aegis turned and continued down the path.

The two walked in silence several more blocks before Kestus realized he was no longer leading the way.

How well does he know the Undercity? He moves through it as if he was born in one of these dark alleyways.

Shuffling through the lower market district, they passed an old vendor hunched over crates of roots and herbs. The street was filled with vendors packed full of panicked townspeople buying all they could. None cared for the medicine this woman offered. Her shop remained empty. Aegis stopped in front of the ragged stall. Its paint was chipped and it could barely stand on its own. A rock was jammed beneath to help level one of the legs. In a fluid motion, the knight dropped a pouch of coins onto the table. The woman blinked in surprise, as if she were unsure of what she was seeing was real, her mouth falling open in shock.

Aegis simply inclined his helm in an elegant nod and moved on. No words. No explanation. No turning back. The vendor snatched up the coin purse with trembling hands, fumbling at the drawstring. A few faces peeked out from behind her—thin, hollow-eyed children trying to climb over one another to get a better look. All their faces lit up as they saw the joy in their mother's dark eyes.

They'll be able to eat tonight. Maybe even for a year, as long as no one takes it from them.

Lips curling into a smile, Kestus jogged forward to

catch up to the kind knight.

"You ever thought of becoming a saint?" He grinned. "I think you'd scare the gods into changing their ways."

No answer came from beneath the steel helm, but his silence held something. The ironclad saint seemed to stand taller, his shadow stretching wider in the dim sunlight of the ruined street.

Crossing through a collapsed tunnel and doubling back near the old glassworks, a Crimson Guard checkpoint loomed like a barricade of exposed bone. Guards in blood-stained cloaks were shaking down everyone entering Knife Point territory —kicking in carts, demanding payment. They were on the hunt, taxing the desperate until nothing remained.

These guards are worse than the ones at the Ivory Row. Those ones at least tried to conceal their evil deeds. These ones want people to see their cruelty. We need to get around them unnoticed.

Noticing Aegis had stopped, Kestus saw the knight staring at him, waiting for a decision.

He wants me to decide what happens to these people.

The thief's shake told the saint all he needed to know.

They couldn't risk everything here. Using the

shadows of the tunnel, Kestus signaled Aegis to follow. Slipping through a loosened grate, they crawled into a sewer tunnel where dripping water slicked their cloaks and dampened their boots. The crawl was short, the stench choking; still, they emerged behind a butcher's stall on the far side of the checkpoint.

No one saw them.

The master thief, Kestus Quickhand, emerges un-scathed... just reeking of shite and feeling even worse for leaving those people behind. Add this to my heroic list of deeds.

Aegis gave no nod, no sign of satisfaction—only strode down the path, onward.

If we keep leaving people behind, who will there be to save? But if we don't stop the King before he summons a fecking god! There won't be anything LEFT to save. Feck, Aegis, I'm trying...

Halfway through the charcoal veins of the ware-house district—where fabric markets had once bloomed before fire gutted them—another check-point waited like a clenched fist, gripping so tight it bled. Unlike the previous one, this check-point was under the King's Decree's control. Their black scarves hung over blood-cracked armor, each breastplate carved with the jagged emblem of their King. Feral. Undisciplined. Not soldiers or men of honor—they were enforcers with too much power and too little reason.

A line of huddled bodies stretched across the alley, people from the smoke-smothered corners of the Undercity shuffling forward, interrogated one by one. The enforcers were working in shifts—some shouting, others grabbing whatever they wanted from their victims.

An old, weary man tried to pull his daughter closer to him, offering what little protection he could, trying to hide her behind his wiry frame. With a cocky laugh, one of the King's Decree shoved forward, pushing him back, mocking him as he fell and yanked the girl into his arms.

"Yea, you looks nice," the man purred, pulling the girl tight against him. "What would you do to help your poor ol' pa?" A mouth of yellow teeth peaked out from under his cracked lips.

A second guard, bald and scarred, drove a boot into the old man's chest, pressing him into the mud, his smile a broken fence. "Ripe! For the pickings she is!"

Aegis froze.

Just a twitch of the shoulder. Barely a motion.

Catching sight of it, Kestus reached out, placing a hand on the giant's armored gauntlet.

"Wait," he whispered. "We do this quietly. We're

too close to the Tartrap. We can't draw unnecessary eyes."

Watching and waiting, Aegis gave no sign of acknowledgment.

Disappearing into the shadows, circling wide beneath a canopy of ash-stained sheets, Kestus aimed to flank the group. Aegis went the opposite direction, threading behind an abandoned cart of coal-slick bricks.

There were five guards. Three at the front of the checkpoint and two above on a tower, with crossbows. With Aegis' size, it made sense for Kestus to deal with the bowmen and leave the other three for the iron golem. Without a word, Kestus was able to see Aegis falling in position as if predicting his plan.

A stone skittered across the cobblestones, clanging against the wooden pillar of the guard tower. Loud enough to draw one enforcer aside.

"Who the hell threw that?" The bald guard standing above the old man snarled, striding toward the cowering civilians. His eyes trembled and widened at the sight of Aegis rising to his full height from the darkness.

Like a shade cutting free, Kestus flew into action. He scurried up the guard tower, the crossbowmen already readying their weapons. The tips of their bolts gleamed—steel, barbed with jagged edges. Bolts designed to tear flesh to shreds and cause even more damage coming out.

Those will tear Aegis apart!

Unsure if these men were named men once—though he doubted it,—Kestusgave them names he would imagine they'd have been given as knights.

"I got the bastard!" One muttered, finger tightening on the trigger. He wore a black cloth around his head to keep his shaggy hair from his eyes.

Sir Blackbolt.

Activating his Shadow Step, Kestus hauled himself up the last stretch of the tower and leapt at the man. He hung in the air a few breaths longer than gravity should allow, the shadows rippling, clutching at him, wrapping the platform in their dark curtain. The shadow of the bolt pressing against the taut string of the crossbow, held in place, refusing to fly. Kestus had stopped it before it could burrow into its target.

"You'll regret this!" He hissed in the face of the sneering Blackbolt. Crow's feet marked the man's close-set eyes, seeming more like trenches, dug from years of age piling atop one another. This was no one Kestus knew, or had ever seen; still, this face was one of many oppressive thugs that believed power gave them a right to stand above those worse off than themselves.

For Kestus, every step was like trudging through a river in boots of stone. The air, like walls of mist, made him strain, burning every muscle, squeezing his lungs. Still he advanced.

Pulling the spearhead dagger from his belt, he sliced the frozen bolt clean in two. With his elbow, he smashed in Blackbolt's nose, cartilage crunching. Then he drove his blade into the man's thigh, knowing the scream would sound like a kettle boiling, Kestus spun to the second guard.

His anger and adrenaline pushed him further, though every intake of breath began to feel as if he were swallowing stones, crushing his insides.

During the past week, Rhyden had driven Kestus to use the bracer during their training. Each time, he had pushed him to hold the Shiftscape's power longer, and each time, it tore at him more and more. His body couldn't adjust to the tug. With every try, it grew harder, straining him worse than the time before. Once, Kestus had tried to force himself through the wall and ended up blacking out, unable to breathe. Luckily, that taught him a valuable lesson. If he couldn't hold the power it would force him out of the *Shadowscape*—rather than leaving him trapped in a slow death. He also learned that using the power in short bursts was far more effective than trying to hold it for long periods.

Stepping up to the second bowman, Kestus noticed this one had spotted him. The man's crossbow wasn't aimed at Aegis—it pointed at the bottom of the guard tower, his brown eyes stuck on the exact spot where the thief had been.

Looks like I got lucky. Sir Bullseye here made me. Unfortunately for you, I can't let you leave this place unharmed.

With a flick of his knife, Kestus cut the string of the crossbow. Peering past the man, he caught sight of another guard standing directly below.

Perfect.

With as much force as his weary body could muster, Kestus shoved Bullseye in the chest. The motion felt like pushing a brick wall. Still it should be enough. For added precaution, he slit the laces of the man's boots, and slashed the back of his knees where the armor didn't cover.

With a sigh, Kestus let go of his *Shadow Step.*

It was as if a hurricane came crashing down. Air whipped past his ears as the screams of the bowmen split the crowd like lightning in the falling rain.

Sir Blackbolt tumbled backward, his head snapping as momentum hurled him from the tower. After a fall like that, it would be a wonder if he ever shot straight again. His bolt shattered in the air, splitting into several splinters that whistled past the checkpoint.

Then Bullseye flailed as Kestus' shove sent him flying, his feet slipping from his boots as he leapt up in pain. The thug below looked up—expression blank—as the falling man came plummeting down, an avalanche of steel and metal. Both lay broken, crumpled in a heap.

Aegis didn't hesitate.

"What the feck is—"

The knight's cloak rippled in a gust of motion, looking as if it were a hand coming to grasp the bald man. Like a figure out of a half-remembered tale, the knight showed every bit like a saint. The guard holding the girl barely braced himself before the armored giant drove a gauntleted fist into the man's temple. The bald man next to the girl's father, swung his blade with the awkward skill of a child wielding a stick. Aegis caught the weapon mid-swing—steel shrieking against steel—before snapping it clean in half. With his other hand, he hammered a fist into the man's spine. Blood sprayed from the thug's mouth as his eyes rolled back.

The two heroes stood victorious just long enough to survey the battlefield.

Dropping from the tower, Kestus' cloak danced in

the wind, showing the people Starstride had come to their aid.

Aegis lifted the woman with one arm and passed her into her father's arms. The man stared, stunned, as Aegis was already leaving them behind, vanishing through the checkpoint with Kestus at his side.

The crowd stood in shock, and then pressed forward in a rush. The father held his daughter tight, ignoring the chaos swirling around him. In just a few brief moments, the people—along with Kestus and Aegis—were long gone.

The thief and the saint once again moved in silence, slipping between alleys and stacks of old breweries. The Undercity twisted around them like a wounded beast. Even now, through fire and ruin, it struggled to breathe.

Glancing at Aegis, Kestus remarked, "You could put Ironfist to shame." Kestus punched softly at the knight's arm. "You made a difference today. A lot of people will be better off for it. No matter how short it may last."

Aegis said nothing.

Kestus swore—just for a moment—he saw the faintest nod.

By nightfall, they reached the edge of Knife Point's territory. The sky above hung heavy with black iron arches, vast and oppressive, their shadows sprawling like the cage of some monstrous beast. Beneath them, the old fishing docks spread outward, broken planks and rotting pylons jutting into the stagnant water like the ribs of a long-dead leviathan.

The Tartrap.

Stepping down into the waiting crowd, Kestus found the air to be thick with salt, smoke, and suspicion. Dozens of eyes fixed on him, hard and untrusting, drawn by something they couldn't name.

CHAPTER 11

The Cursed Hero

The Tartrap was a fortress, disguised as a warehouse. Its doors banded with rusted iron, its walls reinforced with stone and patched in mismatched layers, like scars on old flesh. The entrance bristled with hard-eyed thugs gripping scavenged weapons, axes chipped at the edge, clubs wrapped with nails, and a few mismatched swords too dull to shine in the lamplight.

With a careful stride, Kestus approached, his cloak pulled close, knowing better than to expect a warm welcome—especially with a looming suit of armor at his back.

The first pair of guards moved to block their way, shoulders broad and faces filled with reservation. Their eyes lingered on the outline of blades beneath Kestus' cloak before flicking uneasily toward the steel bulk of Aegis.

"No one gets in without a name, or you show your

bloodmark," Lefty growled, his voice low and rasping, as though he had swallowed gravel.

Chewing his lip, buying himself a moment, Kestus wondered what he should say to them. Then, with deliberate calm, he stepped forward, pushing out his chest and pulling his shoulders back, letting the space between them tighten. His gaze met both men in turn.

"I am Kestus Quickhand."

He let the name hang like a key, waiting to turn a lock. And then he bowed, slowly, elegantly, and a bit cocky.

The two guards exchanged a doubtful glance, before hardening into hostility.

"Who the feck do you think you are? Who do you think we are?!" Righty sneered, his face all puckered up as if he had been eating a lemon. Looking at his hand, apparently he had been.

You don't often see people eating lemons. Where'd Puckerface get a lemon?

Lefty gestured toward a cluster of bruisers lounging by the wall. They didn't try to look threatening; the scars that crisscrossed their skin was enough to tell of their experience—these were hardened warriors, now bouncers with fists that could break bone as easily as wood. "Making things up are we? Well, we've got friends who can help straighten out your crooked tongue."

Aegis shifted closer, pulling back his hood, the faint torchlight glinting along the steel ridges of his helm. His gauntleted hand settled on the pommel of his sword, the sound of iron against leather carrying more threat than words ever could.

The two guards stiffened, hands twitching toward their own weapons. Puckerface dropped his lemon.

The moment stretched taut, brittle and ready to snap.

Then, before Kestus could reply, a sweet, familiar voice melted away the tension. A thick lisp coating her words made them difficult to understand, but it didn't stop her from talking.

"Oi! Let him through, yuh daft bash-turds! Did ye not hear? That'sh bleddy feckin' Keshtush Quickhand Retchet—Undercity'sh Curshed Hero!"

The crowd shifted as a wiry figure shouldered past the guards. She was small, sharp-faced, eyes dancing with mischief. Without hesitation, she seized Kestus by the arm, yanking him forward.

She paused when her gaze landed on Aegis, a grin spreading across her lips, sly and reckless. With a subtle smirk, she blew a kiss toward the ironclad guardian before tugging Kestus along.

"Pouch Grabber?" Kestus couldn't believe his eyes,

slipping a little as he stumbled after her.

Her auburn hair was shorter now, tinged by fire. A small cut from a knife shined beneath her eye. Beyond that, she looked unscathed. Despite her small and thin appearance, Kestus was surprised at the strength she carried. Clearly, her stature had nothing to do with the skill she had; she was fully capable of taking care of herself. The fact she was still alive and the way she tugged him along by the arm proved it.

"Sh-urprised I'm alive, are ye, Quickhand?" she grinned, her missing tooth explaining the whistle. She led him through the entrance and into the crowd of cutthroats and thieves gathered inside the Tartrap.

The warehouse was blackened by soot and resin from decades of use, and with the walls layered in grime, it looked to be the husk of a burned-out forge. It made for a perfect sound-dampener, muffling voices and footsteps, sealing secrets in its smoke-stained ribs. Before, Kestus had thought this place a foolish choice for a gathering. Now, seeing it alive with bodies and whispers, he gave it a second chance.

There is probably no better place in the Undercity to do this. It can quiet the voices of a few hundred men and hide the fire of even more.

He almost laughed, surprised by the sheer number of people crammed into the cavernous room.

Eyes sweeping each and every face, Kestus searched for other Starstriders who might have survived—until his gaze locked on the stage at the far end of the room. It wasn't truly a stage at all, more a landing where two staircases converged into a wide platform that circled the upper level of the building.

"This place is amaz—" His words choked off as Pouch Grabber whirled on him. Fingers hooked around the back of his head, she pulled him forward with startling strength. Her tongue pressed past his lips, brushing against his teeth before she snagged his lower lip between hers in a small bite. She held it, savoring the taste, then pulled away with a grin.

"Uh…" His mouth hung open, breath caught, vision blurring past her smile to the railing above—where he saw Ellia leaning, watching. For a heartbeat, he hoped she didn't see, but then their eyes met. Turning, she vanished somewhere above.

"Aw." Pouch Grabber caught his cheek in one hand and gave him a playful slap. "Few men look pasht the girl shtanding in front of 'em. Sh-he musht've got you good." Her tongue touched the gap in her teeth as she smiled wider. "How about you, Sir

Knight? You look like someone I could get close to.”

Kestus turned, startled to see the iron giant so close. Aegis, however, continued forward toward the staircase, never looking in Pouch Grabber’s or anyone else’s direction.

“Whewf. Not my night then.” She placed a hand on Kestus’ chest, leaning in close, making sure he could hear her through the roar of the crowd. “It ish really good to shee you, Quickhand. There ish shomeone waiting for you up top. I wanted to shee your face but you know me. Gotta mingle. Revolutionsh don’t shtart themshelvesh.”

“Wait!” Grasping her hand, Kestus brought her back to him. Her eyes widened and she giggled. “Before. You called me the Cursed Hero of the Undercity.”

“Yeah?” She blinked, clearly disappointed.

“Why?”

“Oh, ha! Because we all curseh yuh for being shuch a damn good thief! If yuh failed or died, all the poor shorry people could jusht keep acting ash if the shite we were dealing with and the murder and the tyranny wash all okay.”

With a wink and a pat on his shoulder, she slipped back into the press of bodies, greeting and laughing. Her energy was infectious, and with so many frightened and angry people packed into the Tartrap, Kestus could see the value of her efforts. She was living proof that the King couldn't crush the Undercity's spirit, no matter how hard he stomped and tore at it.

Time for me to head up. To play my part. Just like Rhyden asked. Get the Undercity to unite. Luckily, it looks like they were going to do that without me anyway.

He glanced at the railing ahead. Something twisted in his chest—a pang of anxiety he hadn't expected. He wasn't here for Ellia. Still, she had seen him kiss Pouch Grabber.

Stop being ridiculous. Just keep walking and stop overthinking it. She knows it was nothing. Even if it did mean something, it's not like we... Stay focused! I need to see who Pouch Grabber meant. Who is waiting above? Where did Aegis go? The giant was following me all day and suddenly he's off on his own. He's not even going to talk to anyone!

Focusing on each step he made his way up the stairwell. Kestus rubbed his mouth where the sting of a split lip was still lingering. His fingers dancing up the cool metal of the railing, tapping back and forth, he was in awe of how many people actually were there.

Then the crowd below began to shift, as the stage filled with movement. Bodies filled the entire lower level, everyone pushing inward, trying to get the best view. Flocks of RavenHood on the stage above blocked the staircases to prevent anyone else from getting to the second floor.

That's when a heavy silence blanketed the room. One figure strode forward, and their presence alone spoke louder than any words could. Stern dark eyes burned with malice, shaping a face carved by violence and authority.

Darron Ironfist.

The leader of Knife Point stood before them, his massive arms gripping the railing as if the metal itself bent to his will. Dressed in a fine tunic and jerkin with the sigil of Knife Point woven in a bright red, he leaned over the sea of faces, demanding attention before uttering a word. His forehead gleamed in the light where his greying blond hair had receded. Darron Ironfist was not a young man; he was a rare sight in the Undercity gangs, a man in his mid-to-late fifties. With a face that resembled leather, Darron continued to watch the gathered folk. The murmurs of the room withered away until only the echo of breath remained. Kestus, halfway up the stairs, came to a stop without even realizing it, caught in the magnetism Darron exuded.

"They are not ours!" Ironfist's first words were not a call to unity, nor a promise of triumph, but a statement of war.

Uncertainty rippled through the crowd with exchanged glances and furrowed brows.

Ironfist's voice thundered. "The ones who forsake our colors! Our blood! Who once called us brother or sister! Those now serving the King—" He turned and spat, the sound heavy against the metal as it struck. "They are not Knife Point! They are traitors! They are the ones who still believe Alikhan will spare them. Believe that he'll leave them with power over us." His lip curled, his sneer almost a snarl.,"They are fools for trusting the deadliest man in Tare'Envel. Feck the damn bastards!"

His iron fist slammed into the railing. The metal dented beneath the blow, grooves molding around the limb, as though he commanded the steel itself. The crash ignited the crowd like flint and steel.

The gathered criminals erupted, shouting curses at the King's Decree, their fury a rolling wave through the chamber. Names were spoken, as if adding them to a bounty list.

"Needlepoint,

Snatcher,

Mudrat,

Fast Fingers,

Sideswipe,

Downtown..."

The list went on.

This was Ironfist's first strike—severing ties with the faction that had bent the knee. It was brutal, yet necessary. Ironfist had to carve out the rot, he had to scrape the bone, before anyone would trust him again.

"I always thought he was secretly serving the King. Glad to know I was wrong," Kestus muttered under his breath, unease still pressing against his stomach.

Then, another figure stepped onto the stage. Kestus' breath caught. He couldn't believe it. His eyes were burning from staring so hard.

Tyven the Blade was alive.

CHAPTER 12

Great Men And Their Speeches

The Starstride leader was standing with the same effortless confidence he had always carried, though he had a new gash from his throat to his ear. It was a thin and deep cut, still, he persevered. His jaw was as sharp as his blade now, and though only a week had passed, he looked to have lost weight, becoming leaner. More of the 'tactical warrior' etched his stone figure than the gang leader.

Scanning the room, he was gathering the worth of every person present, his eyes gleaming with joy at the sight. When his gaze landed on Kestus, something passed between them—relief, respect, and something close to pride. The man gave Kestus a nod, a faint smile parting his lips.

Starstride lives!

"Hey, Mr. Sh-weat and Sh-alty, whatcha doin' sh-tandin' back here?" Pouch Grabber cut through the RavenHood guards, pulling Kestus the rest of the way up the stairs. She kept holding him, pulling him toward the stag, her arm wrapped around his back as if to stabilize him.

Kestus let her guide him. The joy bubbling inside of his chest was like a pot boiling over; he could feel tears brimming, hot and wet, stinging his eyes. He had not expected the sight of them all—survivors, brothers, sisters—still breathing, still fighting. He had believed them all dead. Wiped away by King Alikhan's hand. Now, to see them alive again awakened something buried within him, something he had nearly forgotten.

Hope.

As they approached the stage, Kestus caught sight of Filko Sharp-Eye eating a lamb keba, and beside him sat his niece, the Shadow's Wing. Filko's glance flicked from Kestus to Pouch Grabber, then back to Tyven and Ironfist. He looked annoyed, as if Kestus was late to something.

"Here we are." Pouch Grabber stopped, placing herself subtly between Kestus and Ellia. She smiled at the other woman.

Unsure of himself, Kestus didn't have time to think or speak before Tyven's voice filled the warehouse.

"For those of you who have not yet made my acquaintance, I am Tyven the Blade of Starstride. And this—" Tyven lifted his blade high, the steel catching the torchlight. "This is *Darkside*. Together, we have answered Ironfist's call. Not as Starstride, nor as vengeful fools. We are just like you. Citizens. Men and women of the Undercity. Tonight we all gather for the same reason. United, the Undercity stands together!"

He lowered *Darkside*, the sword Kestus knew, the one Tyven wielded at the Seventh Star's collapse. His war blade. A similar make to *Starfire*, but this blade held no garnets or design. It was a simple blade, etched by battle, and sharp enough to cut light itself. Sheathing the blade, the fluidity of the motion quick and natural, the way Tyven stood— how he moved—showed him as a swordmaster. His demeanor shifted, the booming bravado softening, his tone now a low and deep baritone. Carrying like a wave across the sea, his voice washed over the people. The crowd leaned in closer, holding their breaths.

"Like so many of you, I lost my home, my kin, and those I called family..." He paused and looked toward the ceiling, his gaze traveling beyond the warehouse, to the stars where the Starstriders believed the dead walked. "One day we will stride side-by-side once more amongst the stars."

Shouts erupted instantly, anger of what was lost echoing off the rafters. Fists shook in the air, voices clashed, the crowd teetering on the edge of breaking apart. Yet Tyven stood unmoving, his presence steady as stone, as he waited. He knew how to control the hearts of men.

When the noise finally ebbed, he spoke again, sharper, firmer.

"Today is not that day. Here and now, we stand to take back what is ours. To take back the Undercity. Our homes. Our lives! To take back Tare'Envel itself!"

The murmurs rose again, hope filling the air—cheers scattered like sparks across the warehouse. Then the sparks caught, spreading into a blaze of applause.

Tyven's eyes looked toward the others. Turning to Darron, the man smiled back, a crooked smile of a crocodile or a jackal. Nodding to Tyven, he clapped in rhythm with the swelling crowd. The Blade turned, waving Filko forward.

With a grunt, the head of RavenHood rose, stepping into the heat of the moment. Tyven looked to the others atop their stage, his eyes shifting from Ellia, to a young girl who sat beside her, then to Pouch Grabber, and finally, to Kestus.

With an intake of breath, Kestus gave the Starstride salute. A raised palm held open like a five sided star, with the other hand balled into fist, and then swung from star to hip.

Tyven grinned, returned the salute and waved Kestus forward.

Unsure of what to do, the thief glanced toward Aegis, and to his chagrin, the iron knight was nowhere to be seen.

Where did that hunk of metal get off to? I thought he came ahead of me.

Turning to Pouch Grabber, he opened his mouth to ask about Aegis, except she was already taking his arm, her other hand pressed against his lower back, shoving him forward.

"Get your arsh-e up there!" She barked.

Looking past Pouch Grabber's head, Kestus caught Ellia's eyes. She nodded in agreement, the green of her gaze glowing like fireflies against the pitch wall behind her. Her lips were painted a dark red, and when his eyes continued to linger, she gave a twisting smirk. He couldn't stop himself from grinning back, dumbfounded, as he stumbled toward the railing.

The sensation was dizzying. His footsteps felt light and airy, his vision hazy, his mind clouded—as though drunk. When he reached the railing, he stepped between Tyven and Filko, and that's when it struck him.

Looking down at the hundreds of faces staring back

—gritty, dirty, desperate—they were all just like him. Undercity born and bred. Raised in the gutters of Tare'Envel and still somehow brave enough, strong enough, to stand against tyranny. To stand against a monarch who would wipe them off the face of the world without any qualms or hesitation. Standing there in front of these people, Kestus realized he had to say something. Of everyone here, there was no reason, it should be him standing amongst these legends.

The most important people of the Undercity. The men who could war with a King... and the thief who caused all this hell.

Filko said nothing to the crowd. He only stared— his sharp eyes sweeping across every soul in the chamber. Then, those penetrating raven eyes of his locked onto Kestus. They bore into him, daring him —asking him all those same questions rattling in his head.

Did you deserve to be here? Why do you get to wield the Shiftscape Bracer? How can a thief be a hero?

It was Ironfist who broke the silence.

"We know who we're up against. The traitors who call themselves the King's Decree. The King's army —the fecking Crimson Guard. The nightmares that stalk our streets, the Hushed. And the worst of the lot—the damn bastard who took my hand!"

Ironfist removed his iron limb and raised his stump high. Flames nearly burst from his mouth in the fury of his voice.

"Alikhan Lorevull dan RosenThorn. The biggest, dumbest bastard of them all!"

Some in the crowd grew still, hesitation brushing through them. If they agreed, if they were even seen standing here, it would cost them everything. To agree with these men meant certain death.

Be it death or liberation, we forge a new beginning.

A hand startled Kestus. Calloused fingers resting on his shoulder, Tyven's voice carried warmth and command.

"I understand. This sounds unbelievable. It seems impossible that we could stop Alikhan." Pausing, Tyven let the tension build. "I hear your doubts. I used to share them. Please believe me, there is hope. For those of you who do not know his face—though all of you have heard the name spoken—"

He turned to Kestus with a fond smile and pulled him forward.

"This is Kestus Quickhand. The thief who broke into the King's vault, stole the Shiftscape Bracer, and revealed King Alikhan the Stern for what he truly is!"

The chamber erupted. Boots thundered on stone.

The crowd stomped, clapped, and whistled for the thief.

Overwhelmed, Kestus stared down at the people, his body light as feathers and his stomach twisted in knots. He caught sight of a little girl sitting atop her father's shoulders, shaking him, pointing excitedly, screaming his name. When her eyes met his, she squealed and waved. Kestus raised a hand back, a lump as big as a boulder in the desert of his throat.

Amid the uproar, Tyven leaned closer to him. "It is good to see you, my friend."

"I knew you weren't dead! Everyone kept saying it. I just knew you made it out though." The words tumbled from the thief, his chest tight with relief. He looked over the gangs gathered, this time with a new perspective—their unity was almost unreal. Like Tyven said, it was unbelievable and impossible. Nevertheless, everything was working out.

Tyven removed his hand, his smile fading into something sharper. He glanced at Filko, though his voice was still for Kestus. "Word is, Rhyden Tuo has his own plan. What is he scheming?"

"He's trying. Rhyden is meeting with the nobles. He believes, with Sebastian Vale's help, they can rally enough houses to join us. But the Captain of the guard may have made that even more difficult for us."

At this, Tyven pondered. His eyes grew harder as a pained smile tugged at his face. "That man and his schemes." He shook his head. "I never could guess why Rhyden did what he did. I just hope he is right in trusting the nobles. We need all the help we can get."

Distracted by something across the chamber, Filko faded away. Kestus followed his raven stare, watching the leader of RavenHood slip into the shadows. As if looking for an excuse, his eyes tugged his vision elsewhere—back to Ellia. She stood near the wall, the smirk long gone. Now, her expression was unreadable. She too was distracted by whatever had caught Filko's attention.

"About time she showed up." Her lips moved, her voice barely audible.

He forced himself to look away. This wasn't about her. She had a mission and so did he. And everything he needed was here. Support. Unity. Tyven lived. The gangs were gathered. The moment was at hand!

With a deep breath, Kestus gripped the railing, leaning as close to the edge as he dared. The cold metal stung against his palms, grounding him in the disorder.

Unbidden, the words flowed out of him.

"We do not stand alone!" His voice cracked with strain, still, his words carried throughout the warehouse, cutting through the sea of noise. Darron gave him a firm look of encouragement, his scarred face stern and approving.

"The High City is rallying with us!" Kestus shouted, forcing power into his voice. "Tare'Envel will stand as one against the King!"

The crowd erupted. A roar like steel grinding against stone, swept through the Undercity. Fists pumped, voices thundered, and for a heartbeat, Kestus felt the full force of their hopes and dreams settle on his shoulders, a coat made from mountains. A burden only the titan Porox could carry.

"I did it." The whisper left his lips, ragged and quivering. The rush slammed into him as if pierced by a spear, sharper than anything he had ever felt before. It left him dizzy, lightheaded, and dazed. "I fecking did it!"

Behind him, Darron continued to bellow to the mob, cursing the King with language that blistered the air. His voice turned the crowd into a storm, driving them toward mania. Ironfist's hulking frame stood to one side, his presence a fortress. He didn't need words—his sheer size urged the people to act. Still, he spoke of taking back the Undercity, pointing the mob toward occupied warehouses where their brothers and sisters rotted in chains. They were arrows waiting to soar.

Turning from the crowd, Kestus spotted Tyven clapping with a tired expression. He gestured Kestus toward some seating, a few benches set up for them with drinks and food for their privilege.

This was the second strike Ironfist had planned. The speeches of the greatest men in the Undercity. The speech was nothing more than a performance and their part was over for now.

Weaving through the knot of gathered figures, some familiar, others he had never seen before, Kestus made his way to where Tyven was sitting.

Maybe after this, I'll take the time to learn who these people are. It never hurts getting to know someone.

Where Ellia had been sitting now a younger girl sat in her place, sharp-eyed and animated. She laughed with Pouch Grabber, their conversation bright and conspiratorial, the kind shared by people who had lived too long with secrets.

As the thief drew closer, the girl's voice became clearer.

"—and there he was, standing with the stupidest face, trying to figure out why he needed to swap uniforms!"

"Really?! It'sh the King'sh palashe!" Pouch Grabber

roared, smacking her knee before slapping the girl's leg. "Of courshe there-sh different guardsh!" She shook with laughter until tears brimmed. "Oh, Keshtush… you desherve better." She grinned, twisting her round face toward Kestus, who stood only a few steps away. The girl looked up, her smirk softening into something warmer.

Sat leaning back on the bench, Tyven's eyes narrowed with amusement. "Word is," he mused, his tone the sound of a blade drawn slowly, "The spy had the thief circling the palace interior. That kind of intel could kill a man—especially in a high-profile job like that. It's a wonder the thief made it at all."

"Shut up!" The girl—the castle spy—blurted, her voice shattering like glass. Color drained from her cheeks as the laughter died around her. Clearly, no one knew the details, except a select few.

Tyven's smirk softened, though his eyes never lost their edge. "All is well, Kwyn. You are RavenHood, sworn by blood. Nothing will take that away. If anyone tried, Talons would be the first by your side. Not even I would want to cross blades with him."

"Kwyn…" Tasting the name, Kestus rolled it around his mouth. He knew the name Talons, a RavenHood of great regard, one as famous as Filko and Ellia even. If she were related to him, it was no wonder she was given such a grand task for her bloodrite.

The girl ducked her head, shadows draping her features. "I'm sorry, Quickhand." Her voice, a whisper on the wind. Her hands twisted the fabric of her trousers, nerves winding her tight.

Frowning, Kestus crouched to her level. "It was your bloodrite," he spoke softly, "and the King's—"

"Not about that." Her words cut him short, bitter with shame.

Unsure what else she could apologize for. Kestus held his silence.

"I lost your cloak!" She breathed out. Her face slick like a stone struck by frost. "Some of the King's bastards took it from me." Rage flickered, curling her lips into a snarl as memory burned through her eyes.

For an instant, Kestus stared. Then laughter rolled out of him, deep and raw. He rose, shaking his head. "You were right to want to burn it. That old thing did what it needed. As you can see, I've got a new one now."

"One already in a poor state. Ill-befitting Quickhand —the King's Bane. Undercity's Cursed Hero."

The words came quiet as a knife, sliding in between his ribs. Ellia's voice. Smooth, deliberate, full of shadow and desire. Kestus turned, drawn to it—as a mosquito is to blood.

She stood near the firelight, draped in black. Her arms were sheathed in boiled leather, her chest studded with throwing knives. A raven-feathered cloak kissed her shoulders, whispering secrets with every shift. Her emerald eyes burned brighter than the flames, locking onto his just before gliding to Tyven.

"Filko spotted some of Alikhan's forces," she informed him, her voice taut as a bowstring.

Tyven rose with grace, dusting off his coat as if this were a game he'd been waiting to play. Stepping beside Kestus, he pulled the thief into a one armed embrace. "About time."

"You were hoping for this?" Kestus asked, confusion pulling at his brow.

"Of course," Tyven shrugged, the motion elegant, as smoke curling out a window. "Ellia and you, well Rhyden, were meant to be seen. She showed her face off, often throughout the streets to catch attention. Then, word of our meeting at the Tartrap spread. The warehouse is large and suspicious, who wouldn't suspect it? Did she not tell you?" Realizing Kestus didn't know, he smiled. "Darron's speech was meant to cause passion—to set the people ablaze. We need them ready. They are our army. Now, let's move into our positions!"

Ellia took Kwyn while Tyven guided Kestus down

the stairs and into the crowd, where the people gave salutes and reached out their hands to touch them. Pouch Grabber nipped at their heels.

What better way to forge unity than in blood and steel?

Tyven turned, catching Darron's eye. The two men shared a look—a silent pact sealed with nothing more than a nod.

"So begins the fall of Alikhan!" Darron growled, his voice booming.

CHAPTER 13

The Thorn And The Blade

The Tartrap trembled—voices thick with tension, resolve, and the bitter history that had kept them divided. For the first time in years, the gangs stood united. The factions that split and fractured the Undercity had finally been melded back together, joined in their hatred against the greatest enemy of all.

Without much effort, Filko descended unnoticed, standing at the entrance of the Tartrap, waiting for his cue.

It is as if all this has been rehearsed.

With a shout from Ironfist, Sharp-Eye opened the doors to the Tartrap and revealed the very people this assembly of cutthroats and killers were so frantic to meet.

"Welcome, my lady." With a very deep and elegant bow, Filko opened the door wide, allowing Captain RosenThorn and her entourage to step into the room.

Unlike before, the Captain did not wear a pristine ivory tunic over her dark engraved armor. Now, she showed the people of the Undercity her true self— a harsh and brutal warrior. The woman who had waged war in her father's name for the past seven years. The woman who had conquered the Voy'Din, and its twenty queens. Blood spattered her garments, dark and deep. Her gauntleted hand rested on her sword's rose pommel, ready to strike at the slightest provocation. The rose-etched helmet had its visor lowered, concealing her eyes, yet Kestus could feel the heat radiating from her presence. She gave a slow, deliberate tilt of her head as she scanned the room. The movement set his nerves on edge.

The guards, previously blocking the staircases, moved into position. The upper rows of the Tartrap brimmed with crossbowmen and archers garbed in raven cloaks, all with sights fixed on the Crimson Guard. Kwyn stood beside Ellia at the corner closest to the door, both focused on their target.

"You just don't listen." RosenThorn's metallic voice rang out. With a laugh, she let out a sound like a bell being smacked with a hammer. "Every last one of you is under arrest for conspiring against your KING!" Her voice broke under the strain of her outrage.

The crowd shifted. Some uncertain, others aching for noble blood.

A figure followed her—a grotesque smile twisting beneath his half-mask.

Sir Loss. The bastard of the Ivory Row.

The King's knight stepped to her side, his armor gleaming as if a feather of Thylarn were in the dim hall. His presence radiated gallantry but Kestus knew he was nothing more than a menace. A stark contrast to Lady RosenThorn, he was a towering behemoth, unstoppable by mortal hands, and she was a nightmare made flesh.

"The King's bitch and her dog. I can't believe you brought that piss-stain here!" Ironfist roared, shoving through the throng. He had strapped on a chestplate and iron bracers. Rage burned in his eyes, brighter than the torchlights that surrounded the wall's. A sneer cut his face as he spat phlegm toward the knight.

The gleaming knight's twisted grin widened, feeding on the hatred that was thick in the air, and growing thicker by the moment. With a growl, Ironfist ripped the hatchet from his belt and leveled it toward Sir Loss.

"When I'm done with you, you'll be missing more than a nose!" Veins bulged in his neck as he snarled, saliva dripping from his teeth like a rabid dog.

"Losing a nose was no great cost...for I have gained so much more!"

The words sent a chill through Kestus. Sir Loss... Broken Nose... No Nose... The Masked Man. The thug who had turned the Seventh Star into a slaughterhouse. The one Kestus had humiliated by cutting off his nose.

His fingers curled around his knives, the cool metal an extension of his hands.

I thought I killed him!

"What was your name before my father honored you?" RosenThorn purred, her voice sharp with cruel delight. She tilted a finger up his chin, then seized the bloodstained mask and ripped it free.

Kestus almost vomited.

They had cauterized the wound where his nose had once been, but the job was crude—flesh blackened and peeling, a jagged stub of burned cartilage protruding from raw, blistered skin. Just below his brows, a piece of bone peaked through. His eyes burned with hatred so fierce, Kestus doubted his knives were enough to kill the man. The beast.

"The Bloodied Skull." The hulking man stood proud, gleaming.

Behind him, a tide of armored mercenaries surged into the hall, blades shining like the night sky. The

King's Decree, in full force, ready to enact their bloody business.

This wasn't an arrest. It was going to be an all out execution.

A cool breeze of midnight air swept through the Tartrap, carrying the scents of sweat, anticipation, and fear. The warehouse felt alive, pulsing—a beast ready to pounce. The taste of battle lingered on the tongue, as if every breath was one heartbeat away from bloodshed.

Crouching down, Kestus felt the thunder that boomed inside of him. The Shiftscape Bracer was calling for him. Telling him to move, to get the first and final strikes. To end it all, with just one use of its power. It was tempting. He could do it too. He had already lived with the guilt of killing Sir Loss, when he was just a broken nosed Knife Point thug. Ending him and the King's daughter would shift the battle. No one else would have to die.

Lifting a hand to halt Kestus, Tyven stepped forward, breaking from the crowd. His movements carried no strain or stiffness from any injuries he may have endured from his last battle against these deviants, only the confidence of a seasoned swordsman.

"Lady RosenThorn," he spoke, unfalteringly. Comfortable even. "You look striking as ever." He bowed, low and deliberate—long enough to show a true respect toward the woman.

With a curtsy of her own, the Captain returned the gesture. "Tyllieum Vendrick," she cooed, a muffled and metallic sound. "My benevolent teacher."

"He feckin' bowed?!" Someone was shouting.

On the other side of the crowd, another person echoed a similar sentiment. "Teacher? What's she feckin mean?"

The grumbles spluttered through the gathered people like a chamber pot spilling on the floor.

Straightening, Tyven gave a smile that never reached his eyes. "We do not need more bloodshed or death here. Tare'Envel has bled enough. Do not harm the people who will one day swear loyalty to you. Who then would you expect to serve?"

"Advice? From the teacher that taught me how to hold a blade and who tried to use me to sheath his sword." She let out a mocking laugh. It sounded as if a crow was crying. "None command me, Tyllieum. If I choose to bleed these people—I will. That is my right! I am their Captain, their princess, their fecking sovereign!" Her words sliced through his plea as a dagger cuts silk.

Tyven nodded, letting a breath linger between them before he spoke again. "Forgive me. I misspoke." Slowly, he reached for *Darkside*. The scrape of steel sang softly as he drew the sword. "Let's settle this without words. Just you and I. Student and teacher. Only our blood must be spilt."

"Ha." RosenThorn's laughter was cold, yet her eyes flicked briefly to the dozens of crossbows leveled at her men. Then to the gangs poised to swarm. It was a miracle none of the people had already attacked, their eyes burned with rage and hatred—their breaths heavy like those of wild animals. When her gaze returned to Tyven, her smirk held no fear; she could see the wisdom in his words.

Tilting his head, Tyven snickered in turn. "Unless… you'd like someone else to stand in your place? A champion that may be better suited to duel."

Though her helm shadowed her expression, Kestus could feel the fire ignite inside her. With a jerk, she tore off her gauntlets, slamming them into the chest of Sir Loss. With a grunt, he stepped forward.

"I will b—" he began, hand closing around his hilt, the other clasping at the armor being shoved into his gut.

"No!" RosenThorn's muffled roar silenced him.

A cool breeze from outside swept in, sending a shiver down Kestus' spine. The moon hung low, peering in through the doorframe, adding its thin, white light to the room.

"Hold these and stay back, dog. If you move again,

I'll have my actual guard pull your leash and put you down!"

"Ha! Not even your new master sees the worth in you!" Darron Ironfist sneered.

A sharp look from Tyven halted Darron's jabs. The hulking man crossed his arms and stepped back, insulted but aware.

This is their plan. End it all with intimidation and provoking a duel.

Yanking off her helmet, RosenThorn thrust it into Sir Loss' arms without breaking her smolder at Tyven. Around them, the crowd instinctively gave space, the tension swelling as if it were the tide guided by the moon.

"Look around you! These are the people you fight for? Beggars, thieves, cutthroats. These people are rubbish. The scum of Tare'Envel. With them gone, we can rebuild. New homes, schools, places of peace. Instead you throw your life away to defy my father. He did not shame you Tyllieum, you did that yourself!"

Dark strands of hair clung to RosenThorn's damp forehead, having beeen pulled into a disheveled tail by her helmet's crushing grip. Her brown eyes blazed with fury, daggers locked onto Tyven's calm, unyielding stance. With a soft flourish—fast as a viper's strike—her blade, the *Thorn,* was in hand. One heartbeat later, she closed the gap.

CLANG!

Steel clashed and sang their song as a hammer striking a forge might, the echo throttling through the Tartrap and pushing the onlookers a step back. Sparks burst between the two. Tyven held his ground, *Darkside* steady, his face serene—while RosenThorn snarled, baring her teeth, her strength driving into him like a storm. She fought with raw passion, with rage so fierce it left an aura following every strike. Tyven was water over stone: calm, unyielding, unbroken. Able to be everywhere at once while remaining still and solid to the ground. RosenThorn was a volcano: unstable and explosive. Unpredictable in her movements, rapidly striking with a force that could shape the earth.

"The Blade and the Thorn," a mesmerized man whispered beside Kestus.

Which will cut deeper?

Pushing her back, Tyven slipped free from an onslaught of attacks, trying to recover, but she came again, faster, her sword arcing high in an overhead slash—a blow meant to break his guard. Steel rang out, as Tyven took the strike and his guard still held. He parried her next attempts with ease—one arm behind his back, his posture taunting her.

The insult burned her.

"You won't beat me!" She tore her blade free from his and slammed it down again. And again. And again. The sound was so deafening, even the Bloodied Skull flinched.

"Aaaaahhhhhh!" RosenThorn's scream shook the ceiling as steel met steel, sparks raining in the dark. "You wish to shame me?! To bring me to your level? Pathetic! You're pathetic! I killed Marriq the Two Handed! Beheaded Yukon the Tongue Stealer. Skinned Xerces the Stone Thrower! I'LL HAVE YOURS TOO!"

Tyven shifted his grip, swapping hands mid-breath. He flexed his fingers, his stance still as ice, though his voice carried a quiet scorn. "The way you hold yourself shames us both. Once, I took pride in naming you my student. Now, I would bury that truth in silence."

"YOU FECKING BASTARD!" she spat, her voice raw from her fury.

In the corner of his eye, Kestus caught movement near the entrance. More Crimson Guards were slipping inside, a growing shadow circling the chaos of the duel. His gut tightened. The crowd hadn't noticed. Every eye was fixed on the duelists and their storm of strikes, parries, and curses.

Taking a closer look at their surroundings, he also noticed that more RavenHood had arrived, and they came in full force. Perched beside every crossbowman stood a raven, black feathers shimmering like oil beneath the faint glow of candles and torches, wings half-spread as though ready to dive into battle. Some of Knife Point's killers had adorned themselves with scraps of armor stolen from fallen Crimson Guards or the King's Decree. Nearly every hand inside the Tartrap gripped a weapon—clubs, curved daggers, swords slick with unforgotten deeds. This had always been the plan —a test of strength, a way to measure the enemy before the dam broke. The enemy seemed to believe them foolish and unprepared; nevertheless, their crimson ranks would learn who stands against them tonight.

Looking for his guardian, Kestus frowned.

Where is Aegis?

His absence left unease knotting in Kestus' stomach. The iron saint's towering figure was nowhere in sight.

CLANG!

RosenThorn struck again, dragging his attention back to the duel.

With a swift thrust, she forced Tyven to pivot left. Her blade flowed like liquid silver, pressing hard, only to shift direction in a sudden arch. She lunged right, blade flashing toward his ribs in a relentless pursuit. Tyven, reading her as if each move had been whispered into his ear, slid his blade vertical and intercepted the blow. Then, with a subtle shift, RosenThorn stopped her assault cold. She twisted her weapon like a serpent striking from a coil and lashed out in a diagonal slash meant to split him open.

Batting the *Thorn* aside with contemptuous ease, Tyven's arm moved like iron forged for war, and with a surge forward, his elbow smashed into the small of her back. The impact cracked through the hush of the crowd.

Gasping, RosenThorn stumbled, but refused to yield. She spun, leaping into a wide arc, her blade screaming through the air, like a predator, diving for its prey. Tyven planted his feet, both hands gripping *Darkside* with a strength that seemed unbreakable. Their blades collided in an explosion of spite and resentment, shrieking as metal ground against metal. The sound sent a tingle crawling down Kestus' spine.

"Enough of this!" Tyven's voice boomed like a war drum.

Stepping back and shifting his stance, it was obvious he would no longer hold back the tempest within. Blade lifted high, he moved so swiftly that Kestus knew he would need the aid of his bracer's power to see it.

Then the blade fell, and with it, *Darkside* sang.

Both hands locking onto her hilt, RosenThorn braced, a scream tearing from her throat as, for the last time, steel met steel. With the force of a falling mountain, Tyven's strike bore down.

Then came the sound—a crack like the sky splitting. The *Thorn* snapped in two like a rose trapped beneath a fallen tree.

Tyven's sword edge carved down her pauldron, biting into the steel and splitting into flesh, drawing a light streak of crimson. The shattered fragment of her sword spun through the air, slicing through her lip and up her cheek, leaving a cut so clean, it looked to have been done with a scalpel. Her white teeth were instantly covered in scarlet as blood gushed out, leaving her with a grotesque, blood-painted smile.

No longer the Thorn. Now, she is nothing but a Wilted Rose."

At that moment, the Tartrap erupted into chaos.

CHAPTER 14

A Fatal Mistake

The Crimson Guard moved as one—a river of scarlet cloaks flooding toward their captain, engulfing her.

"Rip them apart!" Roared Sir Loss, his voice splitting the air as his blade thrust skyward, a beacon of iron fury calling forth the King's Decree.

In that fleeting instant, as his gaze flicked upward, Kestus caught the smallest hesitation in the crossbowmen above. They were waiting for Tyven to move, trying to get a clear shot; however, Tyven's blade was buried deep into RosenThorn's armor, locking them together in a clash of will and steel inside the eye of the storm.

Even amidst the growing chaos, Kestus could see that they were speaking, but he couldn't make out the words. She screamed and roared at the man who used to be her teacher and he yelled at the woman his student had become. In a way, it was their final goodbye.

With a hard jerk, Tyven tore his blade free, a spray of crimson marking its path—too late to avoid RosenThorn's counter. Trying to avoid the onslaught of blows and strikes from the Crimson Guard, she lashed out with her broken sword in a savage arc. Tyvem arrowly dodged the killing blow, blood gushing as the jagged edge carved deep into his left arm.

"Gaahhh!" His cry tore from his throat, the same way the flesh of his skin did—followed by a bellowed command. "Fire!"

The sky answered with death.

Bolts screamed down in an iron rain, hammering into the attackers. The Crimson Guard rushed forward, a shield wall of blood and discipline, wrapping their bodies around RosenThorn with fanatical devotion. They moved like bees defending a queen, unbroken even as bodies toppled beneath them. Screams filled the air—shrill and ragged—from soldiers pinned to the stone, their armor offering no protection.

Through it all, RosenThorn cursed Tyven with every breath, her venomous words carrying only to those close enough to hear. Her broken blade danced with a serpent's grace, as she swung it into every man or woman fool enough to get too close. Her guards dragged her deeper into their fold, shielding her with flesh and steel alike.

The hail of bolts thinned. As each crossbow emptied, a silence, rubbed raw and thin, hung for a moment. It was in that pause when the ravens above began their onslaught.

They descended like wraiths.

Filko Sharp-Eye led his flock, his twin daggers flashing in arcs that spoke whispers of death to every throat and artery they severed. RavenHood fought as if they were a swarm of limbs melded together, their blades darting from every angle, slicing through the King's Decree with ruthless finesse.

Where Filko was the feather, Darron Ironfist was the boulder crashing down a mountain. Hatchet crunching against bone, his iron fist smashing skulls as if they were clay, he was a landslide in motion—unstoppable and merciless.

Sharp-Eye was the sky, Ironfist was the earth, and Tyven was the god who danced between both. He moved, like a shadow incarnate. Even bleeding, his footing never faltered. He flowed between enemies, each step a ripple of precision, each strike a song of execution. The injured arm hung at his side, trembling. Despite the loss of blood and the pain, his eyes burned with an unbroken fire. They held the tears of the oppressed, of the beaten and the broken; their fire was deeper and hotter than that which had burned his home.

Rushing in behind them, weapons gleaming in the blood-streaked light—an ornate dagger glinting in his left hand, his dagger-spear ready in the right, Kestus greeted the King's Decree.

Without a single thought, he vanished.

The Shiftscape Bracer ignited, unfurling an inky black darkness across the Tartrap.

Time fractured. The battle stopped—a shattered mural of chaos suspended in stillness. Limbs hung mid-swing, faces twisted in rage and terror, bolts frozen in their deadly trajectory. Torchlights cast strange images as their fires no longer danced, but held as still as the dead. Kestus' boots made no sound against the stone as he slid through the mania, ducking beneath stiffened arms, vaulting over laid out bodies. Shadows bent with him, bending the fabric of reality as he raced toward the Tartrap's entryway.

If he could cut off the reinforcements, the fight inside would stay in their favor. Capture, not slaughter—that was the plan.

Each breath came light as smoke, effortless. The bracer should have weighed him down, bled his strength dry—but tonight, it felt different.

The realization struck like cold steel.

The Bracer required blood.

And gods, there was enough.

In the edge of his vision, crimson blood didn't just spill—it swam. Droplets of ruby drifted like living things, writhing in the air as though drawn to him.

Tonight, everyone here will drown in scarlet.

Five figures barred the Tartrap entrance—five of the King's Decree, standing sentinel in the archway, wolves before a den.

Eyes narrowing, Kestus studied them. They didn't look like soldiers—no, these were something else, lesser men. Dopplegangers. Pretenders. Hollow fools wrapped in stolen armor, gaunt faces stretched tight over hunger. Their eyes were pits—feral and empty.

Once, perhaps, they had been men of the city. Now, they were beggars playing at warlords, ghosts draped in fine rags and iron they had no right to wear.

The King's Decree. The King's Fools. The King's Fleas. The scraps of the Undercity.

A storm of emotions churned within Kestus, a turmoil so fierce it threatened to tear him apart. These people—traitors, the worst the Undercity had to offer—had sold their honor for coin and blood. And yet, how could he truly condemn them? Hunger drove men to madness. Desperation hollowed out the soul. Perhaps, they only wanted to feed their families, to keep their loved ones breathing one more night. Fear was sharper than any dagger.

But pity changed nothing.

Their reasons didn't matter—not now. If Kestus didn't stop them, they would carve pain and death through everyone in their path. They wouldn't care.

His eyes locked on the first of them. She crouched like a beast ready to spring, her mouth twisted into something that might have been a snarl— or a scream half-pulled from her lungs. The torch clutched in her left hand cast jagged shadows over her face, warping her features into something almost inhuman.

Inhaling slowly, Kestus steadied himself with a deep breath. Then he struck.

His knuckles drove deep into her gut, knowing the breath would rip from her lungs. Then, his spearhead-dagger flashed, slicing through the torch shaft as if it were parchment. The burning brand would tumble, spitting sparks across the stone. With his ornate dagger, he slid between the hilt of her sword and the meat of her palm. One sharp thrust, and steel bit deep into her hand. Her scream would have no air to accompany it.

The second thug stood with his back turned, one hand waving others inside. His head was cocked toward the door, his large nose pointing like an arrow, oblivious to the slaughter unfolding behind him. A club dangled from his belt, forgotten.

In this distorted shadow-state, the stillness made him look almost serene—a man unaware of his own death hanging inches away.

Snatching the club from its loop, he slammed the leather-wrapped wood into Sir Clubnose's fingers where they held tight to the doorframe. Bone crunched under the blow. Then, angling his attack downward, Kestus smashed the man's knee sideways with reckless brutality.

Cause and effect.

That was the gift this realm gave him—clarity sharp enough to cut. Every movement here was deliberate, each choice a stone cast across a still pond, ripples spreading into the world that waited just beyond this single moment in time. A shift to the left might turn a blade's path. A strike to the knee could topple a giant and crush the breath from someone behind him.

He felt like a strategist in the gods' own game, moving pieces across a board only he could see.

The last three stood close together.

Good. It will make this easier. I'm starting to feel the bracer's effects.

Ignoring the fire gnawing at his muscles, Kestus pressed on. The first crouched low, balanced on his toes, coiled to leap at any soul who drew near. Kestus drove his boot into the side of Sir Snake's head with a vicious kick.

Leaping over the crouched figure, Kestus crashed an elbow down into the next thug—the one looming just beside the door. Bone met bone in a dull, satisfying impact between collar and throat. The man would gag—even so, in this warped stillness he loomed in place. Kestus knew that Sir Stone's reaction to his beating would happen so quickly he would probably miss it once he released the bracer's power. Before then, he would remove this man as a threat. Gripping a sword in one hand and a baton in the other, Kestus slid his ornate dagger into Sir Stone's belt, ripped the baton from the thug's grip, then hammered it into the man's right wrist. Something gave. A tendon? Bone? It didn't matter. The thug would crumble, just like the rest of the King's Decree.

Pivoting toward the last of the group, Kestus remained focused.

The Shiftscape Bracer pulsed against his wrist—a steady, merciless rhythm, a metronome counting down the cost of his strength. It wanted more. More pain, more blood, more death! But Kestus wouldn't kill to satisfy it. Pressure bloomed in his chest, as though his ribs might crack from within, a grimace twisting his face.

Just one more! I can keep pushing! Just one more!

With what power he had left, Kestus swung the baton in a brutal bend, busting it across the final thug's face. Too weary, Kestus couldn't make out their features enough to give them a name.

Sir Forever Forgotten.

Dizziness fell over him as if it were a blanket, engulfing him in a silken embrace. The edges of his vision began to blur. Letting go of his Shadow Step, releasing the bracer's power, the world surged around him.

Sounds crashed with deafening speeds like a storm —steel shrieking, voices screaming, the wet slap of blood on stone. Kestus planted his foot behind him, bracing for the whiplash of cause meeting effect.

The first guard folded with a breathless squeal, her snarl collapsing into pain as her torch and sword clattered away in opposite directions. Laying flat on the ground, she would act more as a door stopper now.

The second thug, Sir Clubnose—the door warden —flew backward, ripped from the frame, his body slamming into the wall with bone-jarring force. Teeth fell from his mouth as he slumped over.

The three others came alive in a sudden, savage cascade of violence. Sir Snake careened headlong into the door, skull cracking wood. Sir Stone collapsed, clutching a ruined shoulder, his sword forgotten.

After all that, it was the last one that haunted Kestus.

The baton had shattered Sir Forever Forgotten's skull. One eye bulged grotesquely where bone had caved inward, his head twisted against the door at an angle no man's neck should bend. The impact had broken him—crushed him beyond saving.

Staring, his breath snagging, a sick heat climbed his throat. His stomach threatened to expel its contents.

Porox devour me… no…

Guilt piercing, hot and suffocating, spilled from his chest and up into his eyes. Tears plummeted down his cheeks.

I wasn't supposed to—I didn't mean to…

The words wouldn't come out, silent, unheard. Meaningless. This man was dead. Taken from every life he touched, all because of a fatal mistake.

Suddenly, something vast and cold slid over his scalp. A shadow crept across his face.

Long fingers, threading through his hair like a swarm of spiders—quick and deliberate—slid over waves and curls of a black ocean, before they clamped into a fist of iron.

Head snapping back, the world tilted violently as Kestus' spine wrenched. Stars burst behind his eyes. For a heartbeat, he thought his skull would tear free from his neck.

"Feeehhhhckk!" He bellowed into the chaotic night, as cold steel nestled itself against his throat.

CHAPTER 15

The Giant's Grip

A fire blazed in the darkness of the eyes before him —bloodshot and burning with primal rage. Staring into them sent tendrils of fear through Kestus. The beast leaned into the thief's vision, the glare of a predator savoring the taste of the final moment before the kill. In that instant, it felt as though the night sky had drowned in an ocean of blood, and at the center of that endless crimson stood Sir Loss.

Is he the Bloodied Vessel come to life?

There was no smile. No hint of triumph. Only the endless inevitability of death reflected in those eyes.

Sir Loss no longer looked like the man he pretended to be. He was the savage inside—the shadow behind the name. The Bloodied Skull.

The grip on Kestus' head tightened like a vice, iron fingers squeezing his scalp tighter and tighter. He saw the faint shift in the Skull's massive shoulder, as the knife dug deeper into his neck. Beads of blood dripped down his throat, the warmth wet on his cold skin, the separation of flesh. This was it.

"If you think I won't fight," Kestus hissed through clenched teeth, "you have the wrong thief!"

In the space of a breath, he triggered the Shiftscape Bracer.

The world broke.

The light bled out, and all around him darkness poured in—thick and heavy as oil. The Tartrap dimmed to a void where the torches smoldered like dying embers in a sea of night.

Fingers clawing for his ornate dagger, Kestus glared up at the Bloodied Skull. His defiance grew to anger, and then to rage. He struggled against the beast's grip, but even here, in this warped realm where time bent and shadows curled, the Skull's hold was unyielding—a pillar of flesh and iron that even this cursed power couldn't break.

Then came the pain.

The pressure slammed into Kestus, crushing and suffocating all at once. His lungs clawed for air, but only liquid dread filled them. Each breath came thick, and his hands moved as if beneath black water, every motion unseen, slow and strangled.

His hands were empty—he had lost everything he

was holding when the Skull snatched him. Without the spearhead dagger or the stolen baton, all that was left was the ornate blade. The way his body was contorted, reaching the dagger seemed impossible, but if he didn't the fight would be over.

This won't be the end! I won't die here. Not to him! I just need my dagger!

Fingers searching, Kestus was so close, yet his belt had slipped further away as he struggled.

Feck… Come on… reach.

He could feel the blade at his throat digging in deeper.

Reach!

His fingers brushed steel. At his touch, the dagger seemed to call back—electricity sparking through his veins, a tether of will snapping taut between weapon and wielder. Power crawled over his skin.

"Aaaaahhhhhh!"

With a raw scream, Kestus wrenched against the Skull's grip, muscles screaming, every sinew burning as he dragged his arm through the mire of frozen time. He felt his hair tear as he stretched and the blade drag further across his throat—just enough for his hand to close around the hilt.

The strike came instinctively, almost faster than thought. A white-hot flash—and the dagger was already buried in flesh.

The Bloodied Skull's forearm.

His strength collapsed like a snapped bowstring, making him unsure if he'd released the bracer—or if it had released him.

The world whirled back into focus with a howling of sounds.

Metal clanged against the ground. Droplets of red splashed and coated the floor. A whistle of air tore past Kestus' ear, followed by a cackling that sliced straight through his skull. Then the ground rose up to meet him, his knees cracking against stone. His hair spilled forward, some strands damp and clinging to his skin as if from a cold rain, while others fell to the ground around him. Gasping, choking, one hand went to his throat. Then, Kestus tried to roll away—too slow, too spent.

A thump to the stomach made him curl into a ball.

Blood gleamed in the dim light, bright as molten garnet. It dripped in steady beads down the blade of his ornate dagger, still jutting from the Bloodied Skull's arm. The giant stood, a mad idol pulled from a nightmare, head tilted back in a howl of lunatic joy, holding his wound high for all to see.

"You have tricks, Rat!" he bellowed.

The Skull clamped one meaty fist around the dagger's hilt and yanked it free with a wet, tearing sound. A sheet of blood streaked the white of his uniform in garish red.

Holding the knife aloft, he laughed again—a heavy, broken, jagged laugh—too sharp for any human throat.

"This fecking thing—" his voice cracked into a snarl "—took my nose! You little piece of shit! YOU TOOK MY FECKING NOSE!"

Panic crashed over Kestus. He scrambled backward, boots slipping against the floor, breath coming in ragged bursts. His hands slapped against stone slick with gore, trying to find traction.

With a sudden flick of his arm, the Bloodied Skull hurled the dagger. Flinching, Kestus threw up an arm to shield his face—only for the hilt to smash into his knee, clattering harmlessly to the ground.

Eyes wide, Kestus snatched both blades—the ornate dagger and the spearhead-dagger—just as the Bloodied Skull drew his sword and swept it in a murderous curve.

Sucking in a breath, Kestus vanished.

His Shadow Step, enhanced by the bracer, pulled him through the chaos. The shadow cast by the great sword seemed to grow and resemble more of a scythe. Death had come. Rolling over the stiff body of a fallen member of the King's Decree, Kestus burst free of the Skull's attack by the width of a hair and released the power.

Blood splattered across his face as he stumbled, turning in time to see the Bloodied Skull drive his greatsword through one of his own men, splitting them in two without hesitation.

The man's scream was short, a strangled gurgle, drowned in his own blood before he collapsed in a limp heap at Kestus' feet.

Get up or you're next!

He flew to his feet, lungs burning, legs quivering, it felt like he'd fought forty men already—and still, the tide hadn't broken.

I won't die here.

With a roar that shook the rafters, the Bloodied Skull raised his greatsword high and ran at the thief. The blade came down in a cleaving stroke.

Crossing both daggers, Kestus did his best to block. The impact detonated through his bones, blasting him backward, boots skidding over stone and fallen bodies. He staggered, fighting for balance, trying to ignore the pain.

"Feck this guy..." he spat, wrists screaming under the strain. His grip was failing. The next strike would tear him apart.

His eyes darted frantically, searching for help, for

anyone who could buy him a second more of life—

Tyven had a blood-soaked shirt wrapped tightly around his injured arm; still he fought on, locked in a vicious clash against three members of the King's Decree. Each man lunged at him with wild eagerness, desperate for the glory of slaying the legend. Tyven was far beyond their reach. Controlling the fight like a master conductor, he deflected blades with effortless precision, stepping inside and out of their strikes as if reading their intentions before they even moved. His footwork was poetry—graceful, fluid, and unrelenting. Kestus had seen many fighters in his life, but only one man could move with such lethal elegance, capable of matching Tyven, and that was Rhyden.

Nearby, Sharp-Eye and Ellia, along with their other ravens, were a whirlwind of steel and shadows. They didn't fight with a soldier's code; they struck the way the assassin did. Every engagement was two-on-one, swift and merciless. They gave no quarter, no escape—only a slow blade of death. Their knives kissed throats, pierced ribs, and slipped beneath armor in a dance of murder. For the King's Decree, this wasn't a battle, it was an execution.

Above, the line of crossbowmen thinned. Some joined the combat with steel in hand, while others focused on the entryway, shooting anyone trying to sneak in.

Everyone around Kestus was locked in their own struggle. He knew then—if the Bloodied Skull was to fall, it would be by his own hands.

If I die here, please… don't let Ellia see it.

Kwyn and Pouch Grabber were nowhere in sight. Kestus clung to the hope they had escaped this slaughter, that they had gotten far away from the carnage now consuming the Tartrap. Though each of them would lay their lives down for the cause, Pouch Grabber looked to have barely escaped her last bout. He knew, however, they were all here somewhere, either bleeding or making someone else bleed.

A figure stepped into his path—a Knife Point thug, draped in filthy rags beneath a cracked leather vest. The man hefted a crude bat studded with rusted nails, its surface slick with grim and notched in a few places, yet sturdy. He spat on the weapon and sneered, tilting his head toward Kestus.

"Playing knight now, eh?" His voice was a rasp, his grin full of rotting teeth. "Looks to me like you could use a hand. The name's Nail Biter"

"Thanks. I'm Quickhand." Panting Kestus tried to slow his heart down. The thumping in his veins and the pulsing of his bracer were two colliding forces, off sync, and causing him to shake.

The Bloodied Skull came crashing through the fray, an avalanche of hate, shoving aside a RavenHood fighter without so much as a glance. His greatsword flashed in the torchlight as he hefted the metal and swung for Nail Biter's neck. Barely ducking in time, jerking low, and with a snarl, Nail Biter slammed his nail-studded bat into the Bloodied Skull's ribs with a thunk.

Condemnation pointed the Knife Point man's brows. "I respected you once. I liked your fire. But this? You're killing your brothers! Destroying the family that raised you. Gave you purpose. You've heard Seven Fingers, 'lie, steal, cheat.' We all gotta eat—"

The man's eyes went wide, realizing too late that he had only woken the bear. Unable to pierce through the beast's armor, he had only dented the breastplate; the force of the impact bending the nails around the steel.

The Bloodied Skull's massive grip closed around the bat. Nail Biter yanked. He twisted. He clawed at the handle. Nothing made a difference.

"Nail, let go!" Kestus roared, stumbling forward.

Panic seized the Knife Point man. Seeing the Skull up close, staring him down with the eyes of a demon, he knew he was outmatched. With a strangled cry, he released the bat and turned to flee.

Tears filled his vision as fear filled his heart. He didn't make it two steps, before a heavy boot crushed his spine, slamming him flat against the blood-slick stone of the Tartrap. The Bloodied Skull wrenched the bat free from his armor. And with a terrifying ease, lifted the bat high and swung it down.

The nails parted the skin and met bone.

A wet crunch exploded through the din of battle as the man convulsed, limbs twitching like a broken puppet. His final breath left in a jagged rattle before his chin smacked the ground, his head twisting unnaturally. The bat slipped from the Bloodied Skull's fingers and clattered beside the corpse of its maker.

The Bloodied Skull smirked—an ugly, hungry smirk that split his face like a wound. "Seems someone's always dying for you, Quickhand the Gravedigger."

"I'm fond of the name 'Nose Taker.' Your face is a pleasant reminder of that." Clenching his teeth, he forced the words out through the steady thrum of fear. Kestus had to anger him, push him to lose his focus. In his current state, it was the only way he saw this fight going in his favor.

A harsh, barking laugh came bursting out of the Skull.

Alright, here we fecking go!

Bracing himself. Kestus' fingers turned white

around his daggers. Focusing on the Shiftscape Bracer, willing its power to life, the gem embedded in the dull metal flared as if it were a storm trapped beneath ice, swirling in the shadows. The steady rhythm of its magic rolled through him, calming the edge of fright that was ready to pull him in. Fear lingered—but it was shallow now, a mere ripple on the surface.

The Bloodied Skull was grinning wide enough to show blood-stained teeth. Lifting his greatsword high, both hands gripping the hilt, he was the visage of an executioner. Sweat dripped down Kestus' brow, blurring his vision. He dared not break his stance to wipe it away. One wrong move here meant death.

SCREECH!

Iron shrieked against steel—a sound sharp enough to split a tree. Kestus staggered as a shadow surged past him, colliding with the Bloodied Skull in a detonation of force.

Axe in one hand. A gleaming fist in the other.

CHAPTER 16

Ironfist

Eyes bulging, the Bloodied Skull ground his teeth in rage. His great sword was buried in the wooden shaft of Ironfist's axe, locked tight.

"You're even uglier up close," Darron snorted, and spit directly into the Bloodied Skull's eye.

The monster reeled back, roaring, wiping at his face as if coated in acid. In that instant, Ironfist wrenched the axe upward, dragging the massive sword with it, and swung the weapon down with the gravity of a god.

"Feckin' asshole, I'll be taking more than just your nose!"

Twisting away just in time, the axe tore a chunk from the Skull's side, ripping a hole in the breast-plate.

The counterattack came swift—an uppercut connecting with Darron's jaw like magnets, loosening some of his teeth and knocking the axe from his grip, sending it clattering to the stones. The air flaring out through his nostrils in a grunt, Ironfist lifted his fists. Neither strike was enough to stop either man. With the look in Ironfist's eyes, everyone watching could see he was just getting started. Driving his elbow forward, Darron ducked under a left hook and returned the favor by smashing his fist into the Bloodied Skull's jaw with a noise like splitting stone. The force sent the Bloodied Skull stumbling, his sneer morphing into something more feral.

They circled each other—no swords, no axes, no parley. Just fists, blood, and fury.

Grinning through broken teeth, Darron spat a glob of blood. "Been waiting to put you down for the shite you pulled. You were always too damn hungry. Too conniving. Too damn ambitious. Should've gutted you years ago."

"You gave me my name. Do ye' remember? It was just after yuh broke my nose! I knew then I'd be the one to kill you. To rip off that smug grin you carry and fill you up with steel." Ignoring the spit on his face, the Bloodied Skull let shine the glint of madness in his eye.

Feinting left, then right, he drove a gauntleted punch straight toward Ironfist's ribs. Batting the punch aside, Ironfist slammed his iron hand into the Bloodied Skull's exposed side, driving the breath from his lungs with a harsh, animalistic growl. The thug staggered, gasping like a wounded pup.

"You always thought you could best me? Ha! You're all bark!" Ironfist snarled. With a feint of his own, Darron closed the distance.

Stepping inside the beast's reach, he drew back just as the Bloodied Skull lashed out with a desperate swing. The Skull's fist cut through empty air—then pain exploded! With brutal precision, Ironfist brought his namesake weapon down on the outstretched elbow of the thug, splintering the bone in two.

"GAAHHHH!" The Bloodied Skull shrieked, collapsing onto the blood-slick floor.

Towering over him, Ironfist stared at the broken man. "Like I said. All bark." Twisting his neck to get a better look at his old general, Darron couldn't help but twinge in disgust. "You really are an ugly prick.... This isn't going to do you any favors." Bringing his iron fist down once more, the crack was sickening as the fist smashed into the thug's jaw.

With a strangled whine, the Bloodied Skull rolled to his side, curling feebly into a ball. Despite himself, Kestus felt a pang of pity and horror, his eyes locking on the mangled ruin of the Skull's face.

A jagged shard of bone jutted from his cheek at an unnatural angle, his jaw bent and slack, half-caved in by the iron blow. The Bloodied Skull looked every bit the monster his name promised. Teeth spilled from his mouth, driven out by the gore that ran down his chin in thick ropes. One eye bulged scarlet, the veins burst so violently that the iris floated like a pale island in a sea of red.

The man moaned something, a garbled whisper drowned in blood. Not a word could be understood.

Ironfist knelt slowly, dragging his axe free from the floor. The blade gleaming wet in the dim light as he locked eyes with his broken foe.

"Are you ready, dog? I'm going to put you down," he muttered, voice like gravel. Gripping the weapon in both hands, he slid the hilt into his iron fist for the killing blow.

Quick as a striking viper, the Bloodied Skull sprung.

With a savage kick, he struck Darron's knee, locking him in place. In the same motion, he wrenched his sword up from the ground and drove it deep into Ironfist's hip, just below his breastplate. The blade punched through flesh and sheared bone, the inhuman force of the impact throwing Darron onto his back. In an instant, the Bloodied Skull was on him. Using his shattered arm, he pinned Ironfist's shoulders with an unbridled spite.

"Feck!" Kestus lunged forward to help when two of the King's Decree cut him off. They had been waiting for their time to strike—coyotes circling their prey.

One of them plunged a spear at his chest and Kestus twisted to the side, the steel grazing his ribs as he skidded across the slick floor. Teeth clenched, he leaped at them, slamming his will into the bracer.

The world detonated in a cascade of light.

The Tartrap burned bright as if the sun had torn its way inside. The brilliance was so violent, it seared Kestus' eyes, forcing him to shield his face. Every torch was caught in such a way that the fire seemed to stretch to its full extension, nearly touching the ceiling—begging to escape. Shadows stretched and writhed as if they were living tendrils; sprawling black pools stretching across the stone, readying themselves to claim the dead and the broken.

The room was painted in such contrast, it looked to be from the tale of *Porox and the Black Sea*.

Vision adjusting, Kestus was startled as the final flash faded. A spearwoman, dressed in the King's colors, was suddenly right in front of him. Her stance was unshaken, her grip forged in iron. A warrior monk carved in steel, her long face a serene calm. Sharp angles shaped her furrowed brows, her eyes locked on him, cold and focused. She may have been beautiful once, but with the violence in her heart, he could only see the same hatred that the King spread, reflected in her.

Kestus didn't hesitate.

He slid in low, his spearhead-dagger flashing downward. Steel bit across her knuckles, carving her from forearm to elbow. Her spear would fall, along with curses from her lips. The ornate dagger slid into the gap beneath her breastplate—not deep enough to kill, a cut just deep enough to remove her from the battle.

The second thug was trying to flank Kestus, his long sword gripped loosely in trembling hands. The blade was too big for the young man, his muscles clearly straining under its weight. His face was taut with the effort, veins bulging as he held his breath for the swing. Red faced, his large nose flared with effort.

Keep it simple.

The ornate dagger punched upward into the armpit, sliding between armor plates.

He'll be lucky if he can ever hold a sword again.

Pushing past the two guards, Kestus' vision was swimming from the strain of overusing his Shadow Step. Ahead, the Bloodied Skull was smashing his forehead into Darron's nose. Blood floated in the bracer's fractured time, beads suspended midair—a crimson storm hanging over the battlefield.

I'm too far. Feck. At this rate I'll pass out before I can make it! FECK!

A dozen paces of eternity stretched between Kestus and Ironfist.

I can do it. I can make it. I just have to hurry! Off and on. I can do it.

Letting go of the power, the world snapped back into senseless chaos.

Shadows collapsed, the blinding brilliance vanishing into near-black. His eyes strained as they struggled to adjust. Behind him, screams erupted like a volcano—metal clashing, men dying.

Kestus didn't look back, running with everything he had.

Counting every pace, Kestus forced his aching legs to move faster, every stride a desperate attempt to close the gap. His footing faltered on the wet floor, the blood becoming a sheet of ice; his boots skidding—it was as if the ground itself sought to betray him.

Wrenching his head back once more, the Bloodied Skull slammed it down into Darron's face. A crack split the air, bone on bone echoing like a hammer on anvil. Boots scrabbling, heels scuffing against the ground, Darron had no defense, no leverage—only futile spasms against the hulking beast pinning him down.

Then out of nowhere, a body—thrown from some other savage duel—smashed into Kestus mid-sprint. The collision knocked him from his feet and sent him spinning through the air before gravity claimed him. His back struck a hard stone, the breath yanked from his lungs in a hollow gasp. Head slapping against the floor, stars burst across his vision in a blinding meteor shower. Warmth began trickling from his brow—thin, sticky blood tracing a crooked path down his temple.

Groaning, Kestus forced his eyes to focus, and what he saw sent a terrifying paralysis through his spine. The sight was nearly worse than seeing what the Hushed did to Jeret. The Bloodied Skull hadn't stopped his onslaught, his jaw broken and dangling like meat from a butcher's hook, flailed about as he drove his skull down again and again into Darron's ruined face. Each collision sent a spray of crimson mist drifting through the air, a storm of rain over a dying land.

Trying to rise, Kestus' limbs felt like sacks of wet sand. Helpless, he watched as Darron's arms fell slack, his once mighty frame twitching with each brutal headbutt; jolting as if struck by lightning. His savior—the man who had stood unshaken against the Undercity's worst creature, one of Kestus' own making—now lay on the threshold of death and he could do nothing to help.

The sound broke him. That crunching, the grinding cracks of bone splintering under relentless force—each one stabbed his eardrums with heated needles. He tried to block it out, to think of anything else, but it was all-consuming. The rhythm of destruction, the wet percussion of flesh and bone became the only sound in his world.

Bile flowed into his throat, scorching and sour, he was unable to swallow it back, and it burst out of him. His vision blurred as tears cut paths through the grime and blood caking his face.

He wanted to look away, but he couldn't. He wanted to run, to strike down the monster, yet all he could muster was a crawl.

And then—suddenly—a miracle!

Ironfist's fingers, twisted and battered, closed around the haft of his axe with the strength of a man defying death itself. His grip was so savage it left grooves in the wood, warping the shaft. With a roar torn from the depths of his soul, he wrenched the weapon up and drove it down.

The axe slid into the Bloodied Skull's spine with a wet, resonant thunk. Bone gave way in a shattering crescendo. Kestus could almost feel it—the snapping of vertebrae vibrating in his teeth.

A strangled gurgle choked from the Bloodied Skull's throat as his head lurched forward, vomit and blood erupting in a tide across Darron's mangled face. Then, at last, the beast slumped, a ruined carcass collapsing atop his victim. Both men lay tangled—unmoving, unrecognizable, shattered beyond the remnants of who they once were.

For a moment, the world was silent.

Then a voice—ragged and frantic—tore through the haze. Kestus blinked and saw a man kneeling beside him, shouting words that dissolved into meaningless sound. His ears rang too loud to catch them, the crest on the man's shoulder burned through the blur: RavenHood.

The warrior hauled at his arm, trying to drag him to his feet. Kestus didn't resist. He couldn't. His body was leaden, his mind drowning in shock.

Around them, the battlefield lay broken and still. Steel and bodies, strewn like discarded truths across the Tartrap floor.

This fight was over.

Yet in the hollow of his chest, Kestus felt it—the burden of something far greater pressing down.

The war had only just begun.

CHAPTER 17

Aftermath

The Tartrap reeked of blood, sweat, and piss. The foul stench clung to the air like a curse, heavy and suffocating. Bodies sprawled across the cracked floorboards, some still groaning faintly, and others forever silent, their eyes glossy and unblinking. Pools of crimson seeped between the gaps in the wood, mingling with the grit and grime of the Undercity.

The Crimson Guard and the remnants of the King's Decree had retreated, but their message remained carved into the corpses and the shattered timbers: more blood would be spilled—rivers of it—before this war would be over.

Despite the loss of so many, the Undercity stood together. They had held their own against the King's forces and survived. They were united in their struggles; brothers and sisters in arms.

Ironfist was dead, but the fire he sparked would not

die with him. His people would not let it.

Tyven climbed onto the remains of a splintered crate, his silhouette cutting a sharp figure against the dim torchlight. Blood streaked down one side of his face in dark, jagged lines. His right arm was swathed in torn linen, slick with fresh stains, and yet he never faltered. He was a statue carved from iron—unyielding and unbroken.

"They thought they could break us," Tyven called, his voice deep and raw, carrying through the chamber. The clamor of voices hushed at once. "They thought they could tear us apart before we even had the chance to rise. They thought us weak, something they could grind beneath their boots." His gaze swept over the battered men and women standing in the shadows, bloodied but breathing. "And still… we are here. Still we stand—stronger than iron!"

A cheer thundered through the Tartrap, echoing off the stone walls until it felt like the warehouse itself roared with them.

From the crowd, a man stepped forward, his face swollen and purpled from fresh bruises. One of Knife Point's own, his voice rasped from strain, hoarse from battle cries, yet loud enough for all to hear.

"Ironfist was ruthless at times," the man began. He

paused to cough into his fist and spat blood onto the dusty floor. His eyes glimmered wet beneath the torchlight. "Losing his hand... it broke something inside of him. A lot of us lost pieces of ourselves during that time, some given freely..." His voice cracked. He stared at the nubs of his fingers and then at the broken shape of Darron Ironfist, lying in the shadows. A dirty white cloth, previously covered with an assortment of dishes and drinks, now draped the fallen man's body. The tears came fast then, carving clean tracks through the filth on his face, but he didn't wipe them. He didn't hide how he felt. He stood tall, his chest swelled with pride beneath his stained tunic, even as his thin frame trembled with grief. "But he saw the truth before the end. And now it's time we see it too! He died for it, after all..." He swallowed hard, his throat bobbing. "Knife Point walks with you, Tyven of Starstride. One Tare'Envel!"

An uproar exploded from the crowd, a chant beating like a battle-drum:

"One Tare'Envel! One Tare'Envel!"

Tyven clasped the man's forearm with a soldier's grip, meeting his tear-streaked gaze. "Well said, Seven. I am proud to still be standing here with you." His voice rose, fierce and unshaken. "I'm proud to be standing here, with all of you! Only together can we carve our future." He thrust his fist into the air, and the cry rose with him again:

"One Tare'Envel!"

From the edge of the crowd, another figure emerged, limping heavily. Filko Sharp-Eye. Two men supported him beneath the arms as he hobbled forward, his breath ragged and shallow. His clothes were soaked dark with blood, the fabric split where a blade had tried to end him. Even still, his eyes were sharp, bright as sapphires under the torchlight, sweeping over every soul in the room like a predator that refused to die.

"RavenHood stands," Filko rasped, his voice husky. "We all walk with you, Starstride."

Then Filko waved off his men with a flick of his fingers, straightened with all the strength he could summon, and clasped Tyven's outstretched hand. The gesture sealed something larger than words.

Again, the warehouse erupted—cheers, chants, fists pounding against walls, weapons raised high in salute. The Undercity had its leaders.

The gangs were no longer fractured. They were one army.

"Where is Quickhand? Where is the King's Bane?" Tyven called out, his voice cutting through the mania like a blade.

The room shifted, the chant faltering as heads

turned, searching for him. Kestus barely noticed. The words never reached him. His world was smaller—darker. The sounds of triumph were drowned beneath the pounding in his skull. The blood on his hands clung like tar, sticky and warm, refusing to wipe away. His shoulders slumped under a weight he couldn't name. His eyes fixed on the dead scattered at his feet, and all he could feel was hollow.

A hand slipped into his. Long fingers with black-painted nails, callused while-blissfully soft, belonging to a pale arm streaked with grime. The hand tugged Kestus' gently, coaxing, rather than commanding.

Ellia stood beside him, her face calm, a faint smile resting on her lips—not of joy, but of quiet understanding. She didn't speak; she didn't need to.

Then another hand closed around his other hand. This one was smaller, trembling. It was Kwyn. Her grip was light, but the way she held him felt like an anchor. He heard the faint sound of her sniffling, but she kept her face down, trying to hide tears that glimmered in the light as they fell.

Together, they drew him forward. Toward the light, toward Tyven, toward a future written in blood.

Other hands settled on Kestus's shoulders—hands that did not belong to friends, nor strangers, but to those who shared his loss. Faces swam into view, some dirtied with muck or blood, others hardened with quiet resolve. Their expressions held the same mix: grief tempered by grim acceptance. No words were spoken, yet their intent was clear as they guided him through the press of bodies toward the center of the room.

Ellia broke away to steady Filko, her slender frame bracing the battered raven with a strength that belied her size. His weight leaned heavily on her; even so, she bore it without hesitation. Kwyn slid in between Seven and Tyven, her tear-streaked face lowered, trying—and failing—to mask her sorrow.

Tyven stepped forward, his shadow stretching across the blood-soaked floor. With both hands, he gripped Kestus' shoulders, his palms warm despite the chill settling into the room. He pulled him into a firm embrace, the kind given by warriors who had no illusions of tomorrow.

When Tyven spoke, his voice was like a hammer striking an anvil.

"We all leave here wounded—whether in flesh or spirit. Tonight, Alikhan dealt us a blow that cuts deeper than steel. He has not only taken Darron's life—" a ripple of murmurs passed through the crowd at the name, "—but he dared to shatter our sense of safety. He wants us broken. Afraid. Divided." Tyven's grip tightened on Kestus as his gaze swept the room like fire on dry grass. "I say no. I say we bleed now, so we may never bow again. I say we strike him where he sleeps, tear the roots from his throne, and burn them to ash. If we fail, it will cost us everything. So we must give everything to win!"

A murmuring turned into to a roar of agreement, fury and desperation mingling into one voice. Kestus barely heard it. The words flowed through him like water over stone. He felt empty inside; emptied of everything but the weight of blood on his hands. The dead seemed to stare at him from the corners of his vision, their silent accusations louder than any chant.

Then Ellia's voice reached in and pulled him from his stupor.

"We need to get you out of here!" She knelt at Filko's side, her face drawn tight with worry. The older man's skin was pale, lips cracked, and every breath rasped like sand drug beneath a boot. His tunic was drenched in a scarlet red that had long since darkened to black. The wound—deep, ugly, and far beyond what crude bandages could fix—bled through every layer. If they stayed here, he would die. She knew it and so did Kestus.

She shot him a look that said everything.

Tyven caught it too. He released Kestus, his hands falling to his side. He nodded once, solemn.

"Go with them," Tyven conceded. "Protect them. Keep them breathing, while I gather what remains of our strength. I'll send word to Lord Rhyden—he'll know the time has come." His voice softened, almost reverent. "May the stars guide your steps."

The thief and the swordsman nodded in mutual understanding as Ellia hooked an arm under Filko's and jerked her chin at Kestus. He moved to the other arm. Together, they hauled the gang leader upright. He groaned and his blood-slick boots dragged against the splintered floor as they pushed toward the exit.

The doors groaned open. They stepped from the faint hues of the warehouse into a night awash with the glow of guttering torches and crimson moonlight. Smoke crawled across the streets, thick with the copper tang of slaughter. And there—at the edge of the shadows—stood Aegis, still as carved stone, ringed by the bodies of the Hushed. Their broken forms sprawled like discarded marionettes, their black ichor seeping into the cracks of the street.

Aegis lifted his head, and for a heartbeat, the world was silent.

EPILOGUE

The Bloody Dawn

Dawn crawled across the horizon in slow-burning crimson hues, its first rays cutting through the shifting columns of smoke that still billowed from the Undercity. King Alikhan stood upon the polished marble of his balcony, the stone cold beneath his bare feet. The rising sun painted the haze in a ruby red, staining the kingdom below in a violent, hellish glow—as if the light itself obeyed him. And who was to say it didn't?

Two attendants worked in silent discipline behind him. Silk robes of deep obsidian and rusted gold hung over their arms, waiting. For now, the King stood nearly naked; bandages wrapped around his ribs and stomach in careful layers. A portion of the linen was already dark, still wet where his self-inflicted wound had refused to heal.

Good.

Pain meant clarity. Sacrifice meant progress. Progress meant the pain would be gone soon, forever. Gods do not feel pain.

Alikhan inhaled the smoke-tainted air, letting it fill his lungs, breathing it in as if it were incense in a cathedral. This would pass; the sacrifice of the kingdom would be but a brief moment in the lifespan of a god. Tare'Envel may not even be the first kingdom he would sacrifice for his own gain.

Aware of the footsteps approaching, Alikhan did not turn when his Counselor Doriunn stepped beside him.

"Your Majesty." Despite being behind the King, Doriunn still paused to bow. The length of silence between his introduction and his next words was a direct reflection of how deep a bow it was. "As expected, the old tar refinery held the gathering of the gangs. The report states that Lady RosenThorn struck fiercely before fleeing with her Crimson Guard. The pardoned scum, the King's Decree, is still there finishing off the strays. A desperate last gasp. Fools, every one of them, for thinking you wouldn't be able to find and behead each and every weasel."

Alikhan's eyes remained fixed on the city, except now they held a gleam. Raising the thugs of the Undercity to knighthood was a gamble, a whim, that had paid off.

"Behead the weasel? Your humor has grown darker, Dori. Do keep it up, I enjoy a good jape." Releasing a chuckle, Alikhan quickly braced his side. "Tell me," he winced, feeling the warmth through the bandages coat his fingers. "Have we found the thief, or the scoundrel Tyllieum?"

"Your daughter has yet to return, my liege. She will confirm if our suspicions were correct. Our scouts confirm the thief and Rhyden's companion, the iron knight Aegis, were headed toward the old refinery. As for the swordsman, he was seen sneaking into the warehouse with the other survivors of Starstride. Once the ash cools, our men will recover what remains." Doriunn cleared his throat. "Perhaps, Lady RosenThorn or the devil, Sir Loss, will deliver the Shiftscape Bracer back to your holy hands. Recover it from the fallen corpses of your enemies."

A slow, deep breath swelled the bandages around the King's waist; scarlet seeped through the cloth in a thin line, cooling in the open air. The attendants hesitated, awaiting an acknowledgement from the King's Counselor, before tightening a fresh layer of silk over their king's shoulders.

"With or without the bracer we are still on our path, yes?" Alikhan demanded. "You still speak of this trinket as a necessity, while assuring me it is not. I will have you speak plainly!"

Doriunn blinked, the ire in the King's voice burning as if it were a sudden fire upon his skin. With Alikhan, the line was always blurred. Especially of late.

"As for the rest of the rebellion," The Counselor continued. "We are mere days away from all opposition either surrendering or being utterly stomped out. RavenHood, Starstride and Knife Point will burn." He paused, a thin smile tugging his lips as he looked to the rising smoke of the Undercity and admired the golden light cutting through the ash clouds. "And, by imprisoning Sebastian Vale, we have struck a blow to the noble houses. It was pure brilliance to send men from Lord Vale's army to strike against Lord Rhyden. He would only see betrayal and not know that they acted on the King's orders. The other nobles will fall in line after seeing the two great men destroyed. Fear is a potent leash and you have secured it well."

The King let the words linger. Below the balcony, the city crawled with morning life—caravans stirring, bells chiming, guards flowing like veins beneath his palace. The Undercity, however, moved differently: smoke drifting as if spirits were rising, shadows shifting with whispers of loss.

"Fear," Alikhan repeated softly. "Yes. My grandfather, Ardis the Dusk, would tell me, 'Ali, people are like sticks. They will crack under pressure, whether from you or something else. But if your enemy causes them to break, your rule will crumble. You must be the one to crack the stick. The fear they will have of you—that is where obedience begins.'" Eyes searching through his gardens, a massive obsidian statue caught Alikhan's eye. A stoic pose of his grandfather hefting a moonstone axe, standing amidst a sea of red roses. "Did Rhyden survive the attack?"

"Yes, my grace." Doriunn bowed again, this time he didn't rise. "The man was able to hold the manor and stave off our forces. Nevertheless, the people will see that no matter how powerful they think they are... None can oppose your authority!"

Alikhan's gaze hardened. Gesturing for his advisor to stand, he waved the man closer. Sensing their job complete, the two attendants faded into the King's chamber, to avoid drawing any attention to themselves, while remaining close enough to assist if needed.

"This morning brings only dreadful news, with no answers, or any tangible value!" Alikhan snapped at his advisor, looking away from the gardens to glare at his counselor.

Grey strands weaved like lightning in the man's auburn hair. It was long and pulled back behind his ears, clean and organized—not a single hair strayed or stood out of place, flowing perfectly, layer over layer. The sides of his head were cut short to allow the thickness of his hair to thrive. Usually clean shaven, the man had sprouted a salt and pepper scruff. He had a regal look to him, except for the limp in his leg. Alikhan had never asked what happened to him, for Alikhan did not waste his time with feeble men. Yet, the brown eyes of Doriunn held a wisdom deeper than his forty years of age. They seemed to go beyond even his own years, sometimes frightening Alikhan with the burden they possessed.

"Forgive me, your grace. If it pleases you, the Hushed continue their work. Soon their labors will bear fruit and you will be even closer to your goals." Doriunn took a step closer to his King and without hesitation, began unwrapping the soiled bandages. "You mustn't let this fester. You need your strength for the trials that still lay ahead."

Turning back to the burning horizon, Alikhan let his Counselor work his attendant's duty. There was no warmth in the King's eyes—only the steady gleam of a man staring beyond the visible world and into his dreams. The tightness of the new bandage made Alikhan wince, bringing his mind back.

"All of this," he whispered to Doriunn. "Every death, every betrayal, every fracture of loyalty. It is the soil from which my future grows."

The attendants returned after Doriunn had finished and draped the final piece of the King's ceremonial robe across his shoulders. A black silk fabric, so light it felt as if a cool breeze drifted by when it touched the King's skin. The King lifted his hands, letting them tie the clasps of black beneath his throat.

"Soon you will have crushed all of the rebel's hopes. Everything you have fought and bled for, will be yours!" These were words Doriunn had uttered before, and still, they were the words Alikhan loved to hear.

The King chuckled—a low, resonant sound that seemed to tighten the air around them.

"Hope," Alikhan purred, adjusting his cuffs. "Another tool. Let those fools cling to it. Let them choke on it!"

He stepped toward the shadowed corridor leading back into his chamber.

"Soon they will see that they are nothing more than ants under my boot. Summon my crimson army back to the castle. If they wish to stop me, then their blood will fill the cracks in the granite and give life to my gardens. I will stack their bodies as high as they will go, until I stand on the threshold of the heavens."

Bowing once more, Doriunn fell into step behind his King. "As you wish, Your Grace."

The bloody dawn burned against Alikhan the Stern's back as the attendants closed the great marble doors, showering the King's chamber in shadow.

ACKNOWLEDGEMENT

My sincere thanks to my editor, Christen Ballard, for her insight, patience, and dedication to this story. Her thoughtful feedback and sharp eye helped shape this book into something far stronger than it would have been on its own. I'm deeply grateful for her guidance throughout the process.

BOOKS BY THIS AUTHOR

The Power Of Blood

The Power of Blood is about a thief, Kestus Quickhand, hired to steal an incredible artifact from the bastard of a King's vault. The job seems impossible but what happens next is something far beyond what Kestus had expected. If caught death would be a mercy.
Experience Tare'Envel, a city divided, on the verge of rebellion and destruction.

www.ingramcontent.com/pod-product-compliance
Lightning Source LLC
Chambersburg PA
CBHW071513140726
47997CB00005B/1955